Forever Young and Beautiful

Mount Roxby #2

Aimie Jennison

Forever Young and Beautiful

Copyright © 2015 Aimie Jennison

All rights reserved. No part of this book may be reproduced or transmitted in any form, including electronic or mechanical, without written permission from the publisher, except in the case of brief quotations embodied in critical articles or reviews.

This is a work of fiction. Names, characters, businesses, places, events, and incidents are either the products of the author's imagination or used in a fictitious manner. Any resemblance to actual persons, living or dead, or actual events is purely coincidental. Elle Raven is in no way affiliated with any brands, songs, musicians or artists mentioned in this book.

This book is licensed for your personal enjoyment only. This book may not be re-sold or given away to other people. If you would like to share this book with another person, please purchase an additional copy for each person you share it with. If you are reading this book and did not purchase it, or it was not purchased for your use only, then you should return it to the seller and purchase your own copy. Thank you for respecting the author's work.

Cover design by: Sara Cartwright

Edited by: Kaylene Osborn of Swish Design & Editing

Formatted by: Aimie Jennison

FOREVER YOUNG AND BEAUTIFUL
Mount Roxby Series #2

Beautiful eighteen-year-old Ruby Wilson always wished she'd inherited the werewolf gene like her brothers. They were her father's favourite, leaving her to feel hated, or even worse, like she never even existed.

Once her father took her brothers to live with him in his pack when they reached the age of sixteen, Ruby was left all alone with her heartbroken mother, who turned to drugs and drink, to get through the day.

Realising she needs to get away and accepting her fate she finally starts to settle down and starts to enjoy living as a human among her brothers pack.

Life runs smoothly for a while - until the unthinkable happens.

And life for Ruby will never be the same again.

TABLE OF CONTENTS

A Note For the Reader
Dedication
Prologue
1. An Unexpected Arrival
2. Seedy Bars
3. Bossy Brother
4. Boys' Night Out
5. The Green Eyed Monster
6. Unwanted Gifts
7. Hangover and Flashbacks
8. Meddling Chicks
9. Take One For the Team
10. BBQs and Backyard Cricket
11. Confessions of a First Date
12. Barbarians and Dragons
13. Scarred For Life
14. The One
15. From Heaven to Hell in a Second
16. Pushing the Wolf Down
17. Unexpected Heart to Heart
18. Shopping Makes Hungry Men
19. Blackness Descends
20. Gift From Hell
21. Calling the Enemy
22. The World Shatters
23. Reborn
24. Peeping Tom
25. Hot Tempered Pup
26. Calming the Storm
27. Back to Life
28. Hens. Penises and Revelations

29. The Romance of a Wedding
30. Falling into Place
31. Heroes Don't Always Win
32. Broken Hearted
Excerpt
Coming Soon
Acknowledgements
About the Author
Other Books By Aimie Jennison

A NOTE FOR THE READER

This book has been written using UK English and is set in Australia. I apologise if there are words or phrases you do not understand. Please feel free to contact me at for further explanation, or to discuss the meaning of a particular phrase or word, via my author page or email.

DEDICATION

To anyone who feels like the black sheep of the family.

This is for you.

PROLOGUE
Six months earlier

Considering I'm only seventeen-years-old, I've seen some unspeakable things in my life. You'd probably put it down to having an alpha werewolf for a brother, but you'd be wrong. Humans can be monsters too.

Waking up with a hand making its way up my thigh is nothing new. Sadly enough, I've become accustomed to my mum's boyfriend of the day, or week - if they last that long, trying it on over the years. They always give up attempting to get their sexual appetites fulfilled by my mother, she constantly passes out before they get down to the nitty-gritty. Instead, they prefer to come into my room when I'm asleep and try their luck with me. I guess sleepy is better than comatose. It's not something a seventeen-year-old should have to deal with, but it's been my life for so long now. Just me and my mother. The only reprieve I get is when I spend my holidays with my brothers and their pack.

It takes me a minute or two before I'm fully awake enough to register what's happening. Terry's hand is at the apex of my thighs when I throw my arms out and shove him off the bed and onto the floor. I won't let him take me, her last boyfriend caught me when I had no fight in me. The memory of the smirk he gave me when he realised he'd taken my virginity spurs on the fight in me today. I'll never allow a man to take from me without permission again.

"Get off me, you perv," I yell, not caring whether I wake Mum up or not.

He hits the floor with a grunt, before pulling himself up and coming at me again, the look on his face turns my stomach.

"Come on, sugar. I've seen the way you've been watching me when you don't think anyone is looking."

"I swear, you touch me again and I'll break your nose." I form a fist to show him how serious my threat is, but he laughs and keeps coming. My brothers have both taught me how to look after myself over the years. Living with a werewolf pack can be dangerous if you don't know how to handle yourself in a fight. Werewolves are short tempered creatures, so altercations are always breaking out when you're surrounded by them. In saying that, I've never had to use my fighting skills against a werewolf opponent. It's always the humans.

His hand reaches out to touch my breast and I throw a punch without a second thought. I don't know whether Terry was more surprised that I threw the punch, or that it had actually connected, causing blood to pour from his now broken nose. Forgetting my breast he cups his hands around his nose and glances up at me, the surprise in his eyes suddenly changing to infuriation.

"You little bitch," he screams as he doubles his efforts to get to me. Just as his body wrestles me to the bed, the bedroom door bangs open and my mother storms in.

"What the fuck is going on in here?"

I pause under Terry, taken by surprise that she can even get a full sentence out, let alone see straight, knowing the amount of drugs she's injected into her veins only a short while ago. Seeming just as surprised at my mother's appearance, Terry loosens his grip on me and I quickly take advantage, pushing him away enough to scoot out from under him.

"He was trying to rape me," I say, as I work my way over to my mum. "Just like all your previous loser boyfriends."

"I was not raping you. *You* were trying to seduce me." Terry sounds astonished that I would even suggest such a thing.

"You were in *my* bedroom. You were on top of *me*. And you have a busted nose, how can you say I was seducing you?" I glance at Mum to make sure she doesn't believe the shit he's spewing, only to find her giving me a glare that says she believes every word he's said. "Mum, you don't believe this bullshit? Surely you can see through it, even if you're still high," I plead.

She walks toward me, and I relax thinking she's going to pull me into her embrace. I don't notice the fist by her side until it's too late to block it. I stumble back with the force of her uppercut to my cheek bone. It starts to throb almost immediately. "Mum…?" I whisper, too astonished by her actions to even finish my question.

"Come on Terry baby, let's get you cleaned up," she says dismissing me as she guides him out of the room.

I drop to sit on the bed, unable to process the fact that my mother just took that sleaze ball's word over mine. If it weren't for the throbbing pain in my face, I'd think it was all just a dream. The knowledge that she'd hit me spurs me into action. I can't live like this anymore. I dash around the room filling my backpack with anything I can't bear to leave behind, knowing full well she'll sell anything I do leave. Once I'm packed, I stare at my closed door and wonder how I'm going to leave without another confrontation. I turn and seeing the window, I decide it's the best way to avoid my mother and Terry. Once I have the window open and push out the fly screen, I throw my backpack outside to the ground and climb over the sill, feeling somewhat grateful for being in a single story house.

Picking up my backpack and throwing it over my shoulder, I slowly creep around the house practically holding my breath as I pass the kitchen. I know they're in there, I can hear them. Listening to the noises, I discern she's giving him what he tried to get from me. My anger at my mother doubles as I walk away from the house, knowing they're too preoccupied to hear me leave.

I make it to the end of the street before I realise that although I know where I'm planning on going, I have no idea how I'm going to get there. My brother, Theo's house, is my safe haven. I might be surrounded by dangerous werewolves there, but at least I'll be protected. No one would ever hurt me, not intentionally. Just as I'm passing the bus stop a bus pulls to a halt to let someone off, I jump on board.

I stay on the bus until it reaches its last stop, which luckily, happens to be a short walk from a roadside café and petrol station. The café is a frequent stop for truckies since it's situated nicely on one of the main highways across the country. As I walk into the café, I take note of three trucks that are parked outside. The drivers are all in the café. Two guys are sitting on the main bench that runs the length of one wall, with a good space between the two of them. There's a woman paying for fuel at the counter, if it weren't for her steel toe cap boots and high visibility vest, I wouldn't have guessed she was the third truck driver.

"Thanks, Vera, I'll see you in a couple of days when I come back up," she announces as she walks away from the counter. If she'll be coming back up, that means she's going south. If I don't pluck up the courage to ask her for a lift, I'll miss the chance altogether. The other drivers could be heading north.

"Excuse me," I call out, nervously.

She pauses in the doorway, sucking in a sharp breath and wincing as she glances at me, reminding me of the fact that my face must be bruised up pretty good by now. "Jesus, have you been in the ring with Tyson?"

Her joke eases my nerves and I can only assume that was her aim. "Yeah, something like that," I answer, before asking what I called out to her for in the first place. "Is there any chance I can grab a lift? I'm heading to Mount Roxby if you are going anywhere near there?" I hope she'll take pity on me.

Her smile answers me before her words do. "I drive right past Mount Roxby, I'm happy to have a bit of company for a change. I'm Jules," she says offering her hand.

"Ruby," I reply taking her hand.

***

We'd made good time. Only three hours have passed as Jules pulls to the side of the road just at the entry into Theo's driveway. She insists on dropping me off at the drive and if her truck were smaller, she would drop me off at the door, but the trees are too close to the edge of his driveway.

Opening the cab door, I grab my bag off the cab bed behind the two seats. "Thanks, Jules, you really did save me tonight."

"You've been great company, and you have my number so you can always call if you ever find yourself in a similar situation. Don't just jump in anyone's cab, that's a dangerous game to be playing."

"I don't plan on being stuck in that situation again, but I promise I'll call if I am," I reassure her jumping from the cab. My feet hit the gravel with a thud, forcing a cloud of dust to rise around my feet, visible only because of the truck's headlights.

The walk up the drive takes me a good ten minutes. Theo has a large acreage of land surrounding his house. He doesn't want prying neighbours when he has a pack of werewolves coming and going, which is pretty understandable. When I reach the door, I straighten my backpack and push the little button that is the doorbell.

I see the silhouette of two people approach, but they don't open it immediately. When the door finally opens the sight of my big brother with his caring green eyes before me causes the floodgates to open. I can't hold back the sobs as I pounce into his arms and call him the pet name, I've always used, "Ted."

1. AN UNEXPECTED ARRIVAL
Ruby

I'm humming to myself as I make my way down the stairs with the dirty sheets from Chloe's bed. It took two months for Theo to persuade her that now that The Controller was dead, she was safe in her own home. I think she was just lonely and enjoyed the company here, but no one seems to care what I think.

I'm not one of them so my opinion doesn't matter.

Getting my criminology degree online via Open Universities Australia isn't good enough for Theo. He thinks I need to be working too. And since I can't find a job in town that will allow me to have a bodyguard following me around, he decided to employ me as a cleaner.

In my own home.

I prefer waitressing to cleaning. Back home I worked in a little café, working all the hours I could, mainly to stay clear of Mum and her boyfriends. She knows how to pick an arsehole - then again she doesn't exactly deserve any better. I enjoyed it, though, chatting with the regular customers and sometimes even flirting with them. It's not like I can flirt with the couple of pack members I find cute, Theo would kill them if they so much as breathed in my direction.

Just as I'm about to turn into the laundry, there's a knock on the front door. Throwing the dirty sheets into the laundry, I quickly turn and run for the door, wondering why Theo hadn't unlocked it this morning. No one knocks unless the door is locked, and when it's locked, they will turn the handle until it breaks. *Damn werewolf strength.*

I yank it open, surprised to find that it's not locked. "What's with the knock..." The words die on my lips when I find myself face to face with my mother.

"Have you got a hug for your mum?" she asks. I glance around for any sign of her boyfriend. "Terry isn't here, I left him," she says wiggling a suitcase in her right hand.

Oh God, no.

"Don't just stand there gawking, give me a hug and let me in." I can tell she's annoyed now, even though she's clearly trying to hide it behind a playful tone.

I relax, feeling the heat that only comes off a werewolf's body, as one steps up behind me. "Is everything..." It sounds like Theo is surprised to see Mum too. Gently reaching out, Theo pushes me aside as he steps forward in one smooth movement. "What the hell are you doing here, Mum?"

She drops her suitcase and her eyes well up as she takes my brother in. "Theo?" Reaching out she strokes a shaky finger down his cheek. "It's really you?" she asks before bursting into tears.

Theo glances at me looking as disturbed as I feel. I shrug my shoulders. I really have no idea what's gotten into her. In a resigned gesture, he pulls Mum into his arms and inside the house.

Picking up the suitcase, I close the door and follow them into the lounge. Placing the case on the floor behind the L-shaped sofa, I head into the kitchen and flick the switch on the kettle. We're all going to need a cup of tea to get through whatever conversation is coming. We'd probably rather something stronger, but with Mum being an alcoholic and nasty when she's drunk, it's not a good idea to crank out the good stuff.

By the time I make it to the coffee table with three cups of tea, Theo has Mum comfy on the sofa opposite him. She's wiping at her cheeks with a handful of tissues.

"Thanks," she says as she reaches out taking one of the cups and bringing it to her lips for a quick sip.

Finding my voice, I speak up as I take a seat next to Theo. "What the hell are you doing here Mum? Do you not remember that you *hit* me last time we were in the same room together?" I haven't taken my eyes off her the whole time. I wouldn't believe it if I didn't notice the wounded look appear across her face as clear as day. She's not putting it on either, it seems completely genuine.

"It's something I'll never forget or forgive myself for. It's no excuse, but I was high and when I came to realise what I'd done…it was too late. You'd already left. I needed to get straight. I haven't touched a drop since that night, and I've seen a therapist daily."

Seeing a therapist daily? Yet here she is out of reach of her therapist? She'll have a drink again before this day is out. That's how she works. Beg for forgiveness and then fall back in the bottle again, or even worse - the needle. It's a vicious circle and I've had enough of it. That's why I came to Theo's.

I can't believe she followed me. I stand up ready to leave because I cannot bear to be near this woman.

"Wait, let me finish explaining everything. If you still want nothing to do with me when I'm done, then I'll walk out the door and you'll never have to see me again. I promise."

I glance down at Theo, hoping I'll see something in his face to give me the courage to stick to my guns and leave. Tugging on my hand, he gestures for me to sit back down next to him. "Give her a chance. I'll throw her out myself if she goes back on her promise to leave. Okay?"

I sit with a sigh. "Fine, you've got five minutes."

"Thank you," she says reaching out to grab my hand.

Evading her hand, I grab my tea and bring it up to take a sip. The thought of being all loving and holding Mother's hand, makes my skin crawl, and in return that makes me feel sick to the stomach because a daughter should love her mother. A daughter should want that kind of affection from her mother. What a fucked up mess we are.

"Speaking things through with my therapist has helped me see more clearly where my issues stem from. You're father had his faults, but I loved him dearly. Unfortunately, he always put the pack before me. I was only a human, I wasn't strong enough for him. He never really wanted me as a mate, but when I fell pregnant with Theo and carried him to term, he felt the need to claim me as his mate. He put up with me because I could give him children and hopefully they carried the werewolf gene. You should understand something about that Theo, you never did take Selena as your mate, did you?"

Out the corner of my eye, I see Theo nod his agreement.

She quickly picks up where she left off. "He wasn't a gentle man and he hated that he had to hold back when he was with me. I knew he fucked other women, women who could handle his strength. I didn't kick up a fuss because I didn't want to lose the small part of him that I had. Theo came along, you were my baby and nothing else in the world mattered." The smile on her face was like nothing I'd seen before. It made her look ten years younger and so beautiful. Like a mother that could have been loving had she'd chosen that path.

I can't help but wonder what the hell any of this has got to do with her hitting me?

"Cain and Ruby came along and I felt blessed. Truly blessed, I couldn't care what your father did anymore. I was glad he left me with my babies so he could run the pack. I didn't need him. I only needed you three. My life was bliss, but then Theo you hit puberty, and I realised you were a werewolf like your father. I already had an idea that was the case because you were never sick, not even with a head cold. I denied it for as long as I could, but your father saw these things and once it was time he took you away from me." She wipes at her tears with the back of her hands before blowing her nose into a tissue. "It was painful, God, so painful, but I had Cain and Ruby relying on me. So I carried on, only allowing myself to feel the pain when I was lying alone in bed. Most nights I cried myself to sleep, but by morning I was back to being the best I could be. When he came back for Cain, he broke me. I couldn't pretend like before, even though I knew Ruby needed me. I'd lost two of my babies, and in the process I lost myself in the booze. Being numb to it all was all I cared about." Reaching out she takes my hand in hers.

I can't sit here and listen to this.

Watching the tears stream down her face is going to break me.

I want to stay angry at her. Damn it!

I pull my hand away from hers. "You lost two of your babies and then you pushed the only one you had left, away. What did I do to deserve that? Was it because I was a girl? It felt like you hated me for being the only one there. It wasn't enough that my father hated me because I wasn't a werewolf. No, my mother had to hate me too." The lump in my throat's starting to become painful, making me acutely aware that I either need to leave or break down in front of her. Hearing the crack in my voice, Theo tries pulling me into his side. I almost go, but I quickly come to my senses and remember how pissed I actually am.

Running from the room before I can break down anymore, I leave via the front door, without looking back.

Am I really so unlovable?

2. SEEDY BARS
Eddie

Pulling my car to a stop on Theo's drive, I spot Ruby as she storms out of the house slamming the door behind her. Removing my seatbelt, I open my door ready to go and find out who's upset her. I can clearly hear her sobbing as she runs off blindly down the drive. My phone starts to ring in my pocket and I dig it out as I follow slowly behind her.

"Yo," I answer.

"Eddie, I need you at mine now. Ruby's run off upset and I can't go after her. I need you to find her. It's too dangerous for her to be out there alone."

"No problem, boss. I'd just pulled up as she stormed out. I'm following her now, I won't let her out of my sight."

"Thanks, Eddie." The silence in my ear told me that Theo had hung up after his parting words.

Ruby slowed while I was on the phone, making me only a step behind her as I put it back in my pocket. "What's happened, Ruby?"

"I just want to be alone," she complains, wiping at her eyes before turning to face me.

Seeing the streaks of black makeup on her cheeks I rub them away with my thumb. "Who's made you cry, Rubes?"

"I can't...I don't want to think about it."

She wants a distraction and I'm up for that. I'm good at distractions. Throwing my arm over her shoulders I pull her into my side and start to lead her to the car. "Let's go find a seedy bar to drown our sorrows in."

***

It didn't take long to find the seediest bar in town. Bob's Tavern is one of two human bars in town, it's situated in one of the back streets and looks just as seedy as it is. It may be dirty and full of old men, but no one will bother you while you drink yourself into oblivion. I glance across the table at Ruby, she looks like she has the weight of the world on her tiny shoulders.

"Are you ready to talk yet, beautiful?"

Downing the rest of her drink she waves her empty glass at Bob behind the bar to bring another. "My mum turned up at Theo's...with a suitcase."

Rage races through my blood. I'd seen the state she arrived in, her mother had hurt her terribly. *How can Theo even let her in the house?*

"She's claiming sobriety and begging for forgiveness," she explains not even noticing my rage.

Taking a deep breath, I try to calm myself before speaking. I still can't quite contain the growl behind my words. "Why has that gotten you so upset?"

Her eyes welling with tears, she looks up with a trembling chin. "She explained losing Theo and Cain broke her. I wasn't enough to keep her going. I know my father has always hated me because I wasn't—"

"Here you go sweetheart," Bob interrupts placing a fresh vodka and coke in front of Ruby and taking the empty glass back to the bar.

"He hated me b…because I wasn't like you." The break in her voice tears at my wolf, he becomes restless within me with the need to comfort her, causing me to reach out and hold her hand on the table.

"He couldn't have hated you, beautiful, he probably just didn't know how to connect with a human. I don't believe anybody would be able to hate you."

Giving me a grateful smile she gently squeezes my hand. "Thanks Eddie. That's a nice thought, but I guess we'll never know. It's not like it really matters now, he's dead anyway."

"I'll prove it to ya, drink up!" I nudge her glass in front of her on the table. "You need a night out with the boys, and then you'll know that no one can hate you. Are you up for it?" I challenge.

She looks at me silently. I can practically see her inner debate. A big beautiful smile crosses her face as she picks up her vodka and downs it. "Bring it on," she says slamming the glass on the table.

3. BOSSY BROTHER
Ruby

As we pull into the drive and Eddie parks his car next to Jared's Subaru. I spot Theo standing by the front door with his arms folded across his chest, and I *know* I'm not going to get past without a fight.

"Great, he's got his dad head on. I seriously wonder if he forgets he's my brother and not my dad?" I mutter, getting out the car.

"He's alpha. He only wants you to be safe."

I turn to Eddie. "I'm human, I'm not even pack," I argue.

He gives me a serious look. There's not even a hint of humour in his blue eyes, which is unheard of for Eddie. "You are pack. Anyone of us would die for you, just like we would any other pack member." His last word finishes on a growl.

Knowing I've upset him I feel the need to apologise. "I'm sorry, I didn't mean to piss you off too." Looking at the storm in his eyes, I know it wasn't good enough. His departing grunt only clarifies my thoughts.

Taking a deep breath, I face the inevitable and head over to Theo. Giving me a murderous glare he turns and walks into the house. Knowing I wouldn't dare do anything but follow wherever he's heading. Probably his office.

I take a moment to close the door of his office behind me as he takes a seat on the edge of his desk.

"Running off like that was dangerous. There's a rogue vampire out there leaving dead girls on Dominick's doorstep. Just because he's a vampire doesn't mean you're safe during the day. He could have a human working with him. What the fuck were you thinking, Ruby?"

I have no option but to be completely honest with him. He's a werewolf and can sense a lie, I turn to face him and mumble the last thought that came into my head as I ran off this morning. "Am I really so unlovable?"

Opening his arms, he loses the anger in his body with a sigh. "Come here, sweetheart."

I let him envelope me in his big arms, the feeling instantly relieving my fears.

"It was dangerous, Rubes. You're my baby sister; I don't want anything bad to happen to you." He pauses to kiss me on the top of my head. "You need to promise me that while the rogue vamp is still on the loose, that you won't leave this house without having a pack member with you?"

"I hate being a freaking human," I complain into his chest. "It's a good job I've already planned on going out with the boys tonight."

Pushing me away from his body he looks at my face. No doubt, trying to ascertain if I was being serious. "You're not going out with those guys."

"Eddie invited me and I said yes. It would be rude to go back on my word now." I grin knowing my brother is a man of his word. He would never ask me to go back on mine.

"Eddie!"

The door instantly flies open. Eddie must've been standing on the other side the whole time. If he were a human I would accuse him of eavesdropping, but he's a werewolf, so he could eavesdrop on this conversation from most of the rooms in the house with his acute sense of hearing.

"I can't believe I'm agreeing to this...You do *not* let her out of your sight at all!" Theo orders.

Eddie nods his agreement.

"Wait a minute. What if I need to pee?" I ask in a panic.

"You pretend to be a couple and sneak into the toilets for a quickie. Ed, you turn your back while she pees," he informs me, evidently having it all worked out.

"No way," I demand.

"Then you hold it in because those are my conditions. It's up to you, if you don't agree, you don't go." Turning to Eddie he dismisses any argument I could have. "Who else is going with you?"

"It's just me and Paddy tonight." Eddie shrugs. "We're the only ones not on patrol," he quickly adds.

The frown that crosses Theo's face convinces me he's going to change his mind. I slump into the sofa against the wall.

"I'll pull Matthew and Jared off patrol. The rogue vamp is Dominick's mess, he can send more of his guys out to make up for the loss of my two."

I perk up at his words, offering some advice. "You don't have to lose the use of your guys. Eddie is one of your strongest wolves, I'll be safe with both him and Paddy."

"That's not happening, Ruby. Quit, while you're ahead," Theo says his fists tightening against his thighs, his brow furrowed and his jaw set firm with determination.

Taking in both his and Eddie's determined looks I know I'm not going to get a better offer. "Fine," I quickly agree. I give Theo a quick kiss on the cheek and run off to get ready before he can change his mind.

4. BOYS' NIGHT OUT
Ruby

Smoothing down my skirt I look in the mirror, wondering for the umpteenth time whether it's too short.

"You look gorgeous, Rubes."

Looking up, I meet Bel's eyes in the mirror's reflection, leaning on the doorjamb. "It's not too short?"

Striding over to me she shakes her head as she stops behind me. "You're going to have every males' eyes on you tonight. It'll make the guys' job of watching you a nightmare." She laughs.

I slump down on the bed. "I hate this. I wanted to go out with the guys and have some fun, not turn their night out into a *job*. I hate being a human. If I were a werewolf, I wouldn't need watching. Maybe I should just tell the guys to go without me."

"Rubes." Bel sits beside me, puts her arm around my shoulders and pulls me into her side. "Ed is high up in the ranks, he knew taking you out would mean watching over you and he asked you anyway. You need a night out, if I wasn't working I'd be joining you."

"Are you ready, Rubes?" Hearing Eddie's voice, I jump up and quickly apply some lipstick, taking in my outfit one last time deciding it's too late to change now anyway.

"Have fun and drive those boys mad," Bel says with a wink before glancing at her watch. "I'm going to be late for work if I don't leave now. I want to hear all about your night out, tomorrow." She suddenly disappears before my eyes.

Teleportation would be a fun ability to have.

Making my way down the stairs, I slow my pace as I come to the bottom hoping not to seem too eager. Paddy whistles as I come into view.

"It's about time," Matthew grumbles. Matthew has never really had any time for me, another wolf who feels humans don't deserve the time of day, no doubt. He would've loved my father.

Jared shoves at Matthew's arm. "Shut the fuck up. You wouldn't even have the night off if Ruby wasn't going out."

"I don't have the night off. We're on babysitting duty," he spits the words out with such vehemence, I wonder if he's related to my father.

Grabbing him by the shirt, Jared shoves him across the room. "You know what? We don't need you. Fuck off, go do your normal patrol."

Matthew stares Jared down. He has no hope of winning and he knows it. Looking away he silently storms out of the house. Jared's an alpha werelion, of course Matthew had no hope of winning.

"Theo isn't going to like this." Paddy worries looking at the door Matthew had exited.

"I'll explain things to Theo," Jared reassures Paddy, as he gives me a hug. "You look good, kid," he whispers, kissing my cheek.

"Thanks Jared," I say before he walks off heading in the direction of Theo's office.

Jared has been staying here at Theo's since the night of the rescue. Getting to know him has been great. It's not hard to see the knight, Bel once fell for. If I didn't already have two guys I'm crushing on, I'd easily fall for him too. His blond hair, blue eyes and lean physique are an easy turn on. Although he calls me *'kid'* so I'm pretty sure he's never seen me that way anyway. He's just another brother to add to the ever-growing list of brothers.

***

The club is packed. The guys prefer Misty's over night clubs, but my one hundred percent human status won't allow my entry into Misty's without a specially warded bracelet to negate the entry ward. So taking that into account it's no wonder the guys have done nothing but complain as we barge our way through to the bar. The complaints flow right over my head. All I can concentrate on is my sweaty hand wrapped in Paddy's as he pulls me through the crowd.

Getting served within a minute, Eddie hands me a drink before handing a bottle of beer to each of the others.

Spotting a table become empty as someone walks away, I point in its direction. Nodding his head, Jared leads the way. It's one of those high tables you can either stand at or perch on a stool. Choosing to stand, I push my stool aside, Eddie and Paddy do the same. Jared is the only one who prefers to use the stool.

Placing my purse on the table with my drink after taking a healthy swig, I make my way to an empty spot at the edge of the dance floor. I'm here to party after all and I'm only about a metre away from the guys, so they could quickly reach me if they felt the need for safety reasons.

I lose myself in the music, but it isn't long before someone tugs my back against their hard body. "Hey baby, can I take you on a ride?" He leans down and licks the side of my neck in one long stroke of his tongue. I try to pull away from his iron grip with no luck. "I can give you the best night of your life, all with one little dance."

Judging by his words and actions, he must be a vampire. That meant with one dance and an endorphin-filled bite, I'd be high as a kite and having a blast. I quickly decline his offer, all the while doubling my efforts to break free of his grasp.

Suddenly Eddie is beside me shoving the vampire away with enough power to push a human across the room. Luckily for me the vampire uses his strength to brace himself, or I may have flown across the room too.

Standing his ground, the vampire releases me and turns to face off with Eddie. "Who the fuck do you think you're shoving, you furry fucker?"

"I'm shoving a bloodsucker who has his dirty claws all over a pack member."

Leaning in, the vampire makes a show of sniffing me. "She may be covered in your wolf scent, but she smells all human to me. No trace of a mating to any of you," he says, grinning smugly.

Ed growls and yanks me, pushing me behind him. I'll probably be left with bruises in the morning. "She's the alpha's sister, so you tell the rest of your bloodsucker mates. To. Stay. Fucking. Clear." he emphasises each word.

Raising his hands, the vampire slowly backs away, disappearing into the crowd. "She didn't taste that good anyway," he replies, leaving his words floating around us.

"Fucker," Eddie grumbles as he turns to face me, reaching his hands out to cup my face leaning in close. I lick my lips, unable to take my eyes off his. His other hand touches my neck and I close my eyes, pursing my lips for a kiss. I startle as I feel his fingers brushing over my pulse.

"He didn't bite you?" The question pierces through the lust fogging my mind, and I quickly pop open my eyes pulling back from his hold.

"No, he didn't," I say with a shake of my head.

"Are you sure? You seem…" breaking off mid-sentence, I watch as he inhales. I've been around wolves long enough to know that he's trying to scent something.

Oh God, he's going to pick up my lust. Please let it be mingled in with everyone else's.

"I'm fine, just a little shook up. I could do with a shot or two," I say hoping to distract him.

A smile graces his face making his dimples pop. "That's the best idea I've heard all night. Shots coming right up," he says taking me to the others at the table before heading to the bar.

***

I knock back my drink and tug at Paddy's hand. "Come and dance with me!" I plead.

He shakes his head causing a strand of his dark hair to fall across his forehead, giving me the urge to brush it back into place.

"I don't dance," he says stoically, as his eyes roam the club.

I shrug at his rejection and quickly make my way back to the dance floor before I can follow through on the urge to straighten his hair. I'm on a boy's night out; I can't act like the needy girl coming onto one of them. I'll never be asked to join them again.

"Your loss," I mutter to myself.

I find an empty space and start to sway, losing myself in the music. I can feel bodies brushing up against me, but no one is being inappropriate with their hands. They're probably only too aware of the three sets of eyes on me. They have all been following Theo's orders of not taking their eyes off me all night.

When I feel a set of hands grab and hold my hips, I don't worry about it being some pervert. I know the guys wouldn't let anyone like that touch me, not after the Vampire. It has to be one of them. Probably Eddie. He's been dancing most of the night with one chick or another.

Turning to find a familiar face, I can't hide my look of surprise. "I thought you couldn't dance?"

Grinning mischievously, he tugs me closer against his body. "I said I don't dance, not that I can't dance. After watching those dickheads grinding all over you, I thought I'd better show them how to dance with a lady."

For the rest of the night, Paddy shows me exactly how well he can move.

5. THE GREEN EYED MONSTER
Eddie

Seeing that bloodsucker with his hands on Ruby had me seeing red. I still haven't managed to calm myself completely down, having her face between my hands I wanted to just lean in and kiss her. When I scented her lust, Jesus…my hard on still hasn't gone down. She was most probably lusting over the thought of the vampire bite. We all know how good they can make it feel. I shouldn't even be thinking about her that way, she's only eighteen. Being twenty-two, Theo would have my balls if I ever make a move on her.

I couldn't stand watching her dance with the fucking humans, so I sent Paddy to dance with her. She likes him and he'll look after her, he's strong enough to protect her and Theo will be happy because Paddy isn't a ladies man. He's nineteen much closer to Ruby's age than me.

He's good for her.

It doesn't mean I can stand watching it, though. I've left it to Jared to watch over them as I keep an eye on the exits from the dance floor while dancing with some of the chicks in the club.

The lights in the club flick to bright and then back to dim again indicating last orders. I brace myself as I catch Ruby's scent, knowing she must be coming up behind me. Her hand touches the small of my back, slipping under my shirt and brushing my skin. A rumble leaves my chest as I release the chick I'd been dancing with.

"Are you going to dance with me tonight? Time is running out, even Jared had a dance with me," she speaks into my ear, the feel of her breath covering my body in goosebumps.

Wishing I'd kept a hold of the chick just so I'd have an excuse not to dance with her, and telling my dick to behave, I slowly turn and hold her at arm's length. Having none of that, Ruby stumbles and plasters herself to me. "Jesus Rubes, are you drunk?"

"No, I've only had as much as you guys," she says defensively, her pout makes me want to kiss it away. *Fuck!*

Masking my lecherous thoughts, I laugh. "Yeah, but you don't have the metabolism of a werewolf." Holding her steady against me, I start to sway with the music. "Where did Paddy go?"

"To get me another drink," she slurs. Water is the only thing she'll be drinking from now on. The song finishes and the lights come on.

"Drink up," shouts one of the security guys.

Ruby stumbles in the direction of the table, holding her up I help her along.

"We can't take her back to Theo's in this state. He'll kill us," I state to the boys.

"How the hell did she get this bad? She's been dancing all night," Jared asks taking in her inebriated state.

"She's been keeping up with us. We should've stopped her." I'm pissed at the three of us for letting her get into this state. It's too easy to forget that humans can't hold their liquor like we can.

Reaching into his pocket, Jared pulls out his phone. "I'll message Theo, saying we're staying at your place. I'll spin some story about not wanting to wake Selena and Trudy coming in this late."

"Don't mention that woman, dammit," Ruby grumbles with a deadly glare aimed at Jared. Putting his arm around her shoulders and kissing her temple, Paddy deftly distracts her.

"Come on, Princess, let's head to the car. These two can catch us up," he says leading her out of the club.

Tearing my eyes away from their backs, I turn to look at Jared.

"Follow those two out and get the car started," he says throwing me his car keys. "I'll give Theo a call, he'll be waiting up for us."

I step out the club to find Ruby and Paddy playing tonsil tennis next to Jared's Subaru.

What the fuck?

Storming over, I pull Paddy off her by the scruff of his neck and shove him against the car with a growl. "What the fuck, are you doing? She's plastered and you're taking advantage of her, you fucking dick."

He lowers his eyes in submission, no doubt realising how wrong he was to be caught in that position.

Ruby tugs at the back of my shirt. "We were just making out. You've been doing it with chicks all night. Get over it, Eddie,"

"Come on sweetheart, let's get in the car and leave these two to their little fight," Jared says as I feel him pulling her away from us.

"She's having my room tonight. You're not going anywhere near her until she's sober, even in the car." I push away from him, not caring how hard I do it.

"Anyone would think you have a thing for her," he mutters as he opens the passenger door.

They'd be fucking right, a voice in my head says.

Ignoring his comment *and* the voice in my head, I slide into the back of the car next to Ruby, who's snoring with her head leaning against the window.

Only a few minutes pass and Jared pulls to a stop outside our two-bedroom duplex. Paddy exits the car silently and heads straight to unlock the door, as I walk around the car and pick up our sleeping beauty.

Carrying her into my bedroom, I place her gently on the king size bed. Stepping back I take in the sight before me. She looks so small on my bed but so perfect, like she belongs there. My wolf is more than happy with her being there, he's nudging me to join her. It takes all my willpower to ignore him and turn away from her.

It surprises me to find Jared standing in the doorway with his arms folded across his chest. "You want her!" His words a statement, not a question.

"I can't have her. I'm too old for her and I'm a player, no one would let me near her," I say hoping to end the conversation with my blatant honesty.

He shakes his head. "You're a good guy, Ed, and you're only what...four years older? That's not too old."

"She has a thing for Paddy, so it's pointless even discussing it." I edge forward to leave the room forcing Jared to step back into the hallway to give me space to close the door behind us.

We hear Ruby moan through the closed door. "Eddie, I think I'm going to be sick."

"Look after her, she's going to need it. Is there anything I can get you?" he offers as he starts down the hallway.

"No, we don't have any paracetamol, we never need the stuff," I say as I quickly grab a bucket from the bathroom, which is just across the hall from my room. Paddy likes to try and save water by placing it in the bottom of the shower when he uses it. It just pisses me off and gets under my feet, I usually end up kicking it over, so he hardly ever gets to pour it on the plants like he means to.

Placing the bucket beside the bed I sit down. Holding her hair back with one hand, I rub gentle circles on Ruby's back with the other as she vomits over the edge of the bed and into the bucket. Once she's emptied her stomach she lays back and closes her eyes with a whimper. I watch for a minute and when her breathing evens out I get up and take the bucket to quickly clean it out before she needs it again.

"I like you too, Eddie," she mutters.

6. UNWANTED GIFTS
Dominick

Closing the door to my private quarters, I breathe a sigh of relief. Today has been a harrowing day. Being The King has its drawbacks some days. Thankfully once the younger vampires die for the day, I finally get a reprieve before I have to turn in myself.

A knock on the door tells me I'm getting no respite today. "I hope it's important because you know your life isn't worth anything less," I call through the door.

"I'm sorry to disturb you, sir. But there's been an unexpected delivery," Niko my head of security announces as he opens the door and enters, carrying what looks like a young girl's body hung over his shoulder. The lack of heartbeat tells me she's dead. It's the third body I've been gifted in as many weeks.

I sigh and ask a question I already know the answer to. "Let me guess, nobody saw him?"

"Not a thing," Niko answers with a shake of his head.

"What's he getting from this?" I ask, not really needing an answer because it's obvious. He's getting a kick out of pissing me off.

"He's getting a nice fill while he drives you crazy as he disrespects your laws," Niko answers me regardless, dropping the body to the floor with a thud. We don't have many laws but not killing for food is one of our oldest and most important ones.

"I wasn't in need of an answer Niklaus."

"Sorry."

I dismiss his apology with a wave of my hand as I crouch over the body. A single bite to the artery; completely drained; late teens; blonde. I pull her eyelid back to see her eyes are green just like the others. I don't know why I even bother looking.

"I think we can officially say he has a type."

Leaning as close to the wound as possible, I try to catch his scent hoping to recognise it so he can be stopped before another innocent life is ended. I know how addictive it is to drain a body completely, there's nothing like drowning in someone's life force, and when you hit that point of no return…The laws are there for a reason, could you imagine if we were all free to kill when we feed? We'd start to run out of humans in no time.

"Do the usual. Disguise the wound and put her somewhere she'll be found." A beautiful young thing like this is bound to have someone missing her. It's better that they find her and be placated with some explanation of what happened to her, rather than be searching for a missing person and digging for anything they can find.

Niko picks up the girl with a nod and leaves without a word. He still has a short time before he's dead for the day. The older we are, the longer we can last, but like humans we need sleep to recuperate. He'll most likely do the job himself leaving his feeder to just dispose of her. He's one of my most loyal men. I didn't sire him, so he has no real tie to me but he's as loyal as any vampire I've turned myself. Even more so. Niklaus has been by my side for a long time. He's never left, even after he turned his lover over one hundred and fifty years ago.

As I close the door behind me, I pull my phone out of my pocket and make my way to my desk perching against it. I hit call on the relevant number and put the phone to my ear as I wait for an answer.

"To what do I owe the honour that the head bloodsucker called me himself?" Theo answers as snarkily as ever. I thought our recent fight against The Controller had brought us closer together. I guess I was wrong.

"I'm in no mood to bite, Theo. He's killed again. Same MO. And I'm no closer to finding him. He's good at covering his tracks, but he's getting braver and dumping them closer. Someone is bound to catch him soon," I explain getting right to the point.

Theo's voice thunders down the line. "Soon isn't good enough, Drake!"

"Tell me, what have your wolves found, Wilson," I snap, addressing him by his surname as he had me. I take a moment of his silence to calm myself down. Not enough to stop myself making a remark. "I thought as much."

He sighs. "Fine. But just because neither of us is close to pinning him down, doesn't mean we have time to waste. The longer this takes, more innocents die. That is unacceptable," Theo admonishes as if I don't already now this.

"Do you think I don't care about that?" I don't give him time to answer, pausing for just a second before carrying on, "Just because my morals are different to yours, it doesn't mean I'm completely heartless."

"Huh..." he pauses as if not knowing exactly how to reply, before carrying on without acknowledging my previous statement, "Thanks for updating me. I'll make sure my guys search harder." He hangs up without saying goodbye. *And people call me rude. I deserved an apology there.*

Throwing my phone on the desk I make my way to the king size bed, getting comfortable before calling my feeder in. "Sam, send Gerry in now." I don't raise my voice knowing Sam will hear me well enough with her acute vampire hearing.

Only a couple of minutes passes before my tall, dark, handsome, feeder and lover for the night enters the room, closing and locking the door behind him.

7. HANGOVERS AND FLASHBACKS
Ruby

Someone's going at my skull with an ice pick. I try to lift my head off the pillow and instantly regret it; the ice pick becomes even more persistent. Grabbing my head to secure it in my hands, I can't help but groan.

If I survive this, I'm never drinking again.

The door bursts open and I turn my head to find Eddie barraging into the room, wearing just a towel around his waist and shaving cream on his face. His ginger hair looks almost brown, wet with the water from his shower.

"Jesus, I thought you were dying."

Even the sight of him practically naked doesn't take my mind off the hammering in my skull. "I am," I complain as I squeeze my eyes shut hoping to ease the pain.

"How are you feeling, beautiful? Do you need some painkillers?" he asks from beside me. I feel the bed dip as he sits beside my legs. He's almost naked next to me on the bed and he's as cool as a cucumber.

Freaking werewolves and their immunity to embarrassment over nudity.

Taking a breath to calm my hormones, I gulp in the smell of food coming through the now open door. "Oh my God! What's that smell? I think…" My stomach heaves at the smell stopping me mid-sentence.

Seeing my predicament, Eddie pulls me to the edge of the bed where I can see a bucket strategically placed on the floor. I lose what little I have left in my stomach while Eddie holds my hair and strokes my back. I vaguely flash to something similar happening throughout the night.

Did he really look after me all night?

"Do you think you could keep some painkillers down?" he asks still stroking gentle circles on my back. I grimace at the thought of swallowing anything.

"I think I have some *Alka-Seltzer* in my handbag, they should settle my stomach and ease my head," I answer as I close my eyes and enjoy the comfort of him rubbing my back.

His hand stops and his weight lifts off the bed. "I'll see where your bag got to. It might have been left in the car." I hear his footsteps pad through the room before the door closes with a click and all goes quiet again.

I shuffle just enough to lay my head on the side of the bed, rather than having it hanging over the edge and close my eyes as I wait for Eddie to come back.

I wake up to find a glass of water and a double packet of *Alka-Seltzer* on the bedside table. I have no idea how much time has passed since Eddie left. Moving slowly, trying not to set the ice pick to the skull again, I sit up and mix the tablets with the water, drinking it down when it stops fizzing.

Feeling marginally better, I decide to find the others, after a visit to the bathroom. I really need to brush my teeth even if it's only with my finger. It doesn't take me long to freshen up, and I'm soon walking into the lounge to look for the guys.

"Eddie? Paddy?" I call out as I walk through the duplex. Seeing no sign of anyone. Looking at my watch I notice it's ten in the morning. I open my mouth to call again as Paddy comes in through a door leading outside from the kitchen.

"Hey, Sleeping Beauty has woken up," he says as he reaches into the fridge, pulling out a bottle of orange juice.

"How're you feeling?" Jared asks as he enters through the same door and stops to lean his back against the worktop.

I grimace at the sight of the acidic orange juice. "I'm okay, it's nothing a glass of lemonade and a packet of plain chips can't sort out. I guess Mum managed to teach me a few things in her drunken predicaments." It's ironic really; in my anger at my mum I went and did one of the things I hate her for. Turned to the booze. I don't think I could feel anymore disgusted with myself.

Obviously putting two and two together Jared pulls me into a hug. "You're not a drunk, sweetheart, you just had a night out and let loose. We all need to do it sometimes." Kissing me on the top of the head he releases me.

"Where's Eddie? I think I owe him a thank you for staying with my vomiting arse last night," I say as I peer around, thinking his name will conjure him. Werewolves tend to turn up when they hear their names, even if they've been in an entirely different part of the house.

"He had to go to work. He'll probably turn up at Theo's later, you'll be able to thank him then," Paddy says distractedly as he roots through the fridge. "Aha! I knew we had one in here somewhere. Here…" he says pulling a can of lemonade out and holding it out in front of me.

I take the can and tap the top before popping it open. "Thank you."

"There're some chips in the pantry if you want some, the plain ones never get eaten."

Looking in the pantry I see plenty of plain bags. Grabbing the bag that's closest to me, I shut the pantry and sit at the breakfast bar settling in to try and cure my hangover.

Jared talks over my munching. "I called Theo last night and spun some shit about not wanting to wake up Trudy and Selena. That's why we slept here. I don't think he believed a word of it so be prepared for the papa wolf lecture."

"I'm always prepared for one of those, he gives me one on a daily basis," I say with a laugh.

Jared laughs. "Yeah, I've noticed he likes to father you," Jared admits. He's been living with us since he arrived in town, he'd have to be blind not to have noticed.

"I think he's trying to make up for the fact that our father didn't want anything to do with me. He's just attempting to be the father figure I never had. Unfortunately, he forgets I'm eighteen. I've managed so far, I don't really need a father now." I stand as I finish my last mouthful of chips.

Paddy takes my rubbish and throws it across the room and into the bin. "He's the alpha, he fathers us all," he says nonchalantly,

"Let's go face the music then," I state walking out the room, heading for the front door and car, knowing now is as good a time as any.

***

Paddy reaches past me to open the car door, giving me an eerie déjà vu moment. *Oh, shit!* Scratch that, it's a flashback from last night. I kissed one of my crushes hours ago and I'm only just remembering it now.

Our mouths coming together in a kiss before my hands roamed over his chest and around his neck.

"We kissed?" I ask stunned.

He reaches his hand up and rubs at the back of his neck, looking sheepish. "Yeah, I'm sorry about that."

"The details are a bit fuzzy, but I'm pretty sure I should be apologising. I threw myself at you," I say.

Another flashback hits, *Eddie enraged and pinning Paddy to the car.*

I groan as I slide into the front seat and Paddy shuts the door, before slipping into the back. "Eddie practically bit your head off. I'm so sorry."

On the drive home, I can't help but dwell on what an idiot I was last night. I drank myself into oblivion, threw myself at Paddy and then finished the night off by throwing up in front of Eddie, all because my drunk of a mother turned up on Theo's doorstep sober. Maybe if she really is sober and seeing a therapist, she deserves a second chance. I think I owe a few apologies.

Jared turns off the engine, tearing me away from my inner musings. "Are you okay, Ruby? You were awfully quiet on the drive down here."

I turn to find him looking at me, his eyes full of concern. "Yeah, I'm good. I was just deciding who I should apologise to first, the list is endless."

"I don't need one and neither does Jared. So you're all square in here," Paddy says exiting the car. Both Jared and I follow his lead and head for the house.

The front door bursts open before any of us are even close.

"Ruby, how are you?" I can hear the worry in my mother's voice as she runs down the steps. I glance at Jared next to me searching for a way to dodge her. My thoughts from the car journey come back to me, *I need to give her a second chance.*

"I'm fine, Mum," I reply, trying not to flinch as she pulls me into a hug. I'm not used to her cuddling me, she's usually throwing punches in a drunken rage.

"Eddie came by earlier and told us you weren't feeling too good," she says squeezing me so hard I can barely breathe.

"Mum, let her breathe. It was a hangover, she'll be fine," Theo commands, as he tugs her off me.

Marching to the house on a mission, she shouts over her shoulder, "I know how to deal with a hangover. Chips and lemonade will have you feeling right in no time."

"Mum, I've alread—"

Theo grabs my arm interrupting my words. "Let her do it. She wants to make things up to you. We had a long talk last night and she really does mean it. There was no lie behind her words. I took her into town to see her new therapist this morning."

I follow her into the house with a sigh. If she's really trying, the least I can do is eat another bag of chips.

Before I can get too far away, Theo's arm falls over my shoulders. "Not so fast, missy. What the hell were you thinking trying to keep up with the boys last night?" He directs me into the house and through to the lounge.

"I wasn't thinking, I was drinking and I've been paying for it. What with vomiting and the flashbacks? I don't think you could give me anything worse as a punishment."

He grunts as though he appreciates my self-imposed punishment. "Don't do it again or I won't be able to trust you to go out in the future."

"I'm an adult, Theo, you can't treat me like a kid forever," I admonish, moving out from under his arm.

"You'll always be my kid sister. Even when you're fifty and look twice as old as I do," he says planting a kiss on my temple before allowing me to step away. Another reason I wouldn't mind being a werewolf like my brother. I'm going to grow old as everyone around me stays looking like they're in their mid-twenties. Damn that werewolf gene and it prolonging their lives.

8. Meddling Chicks
Eddie

Concentrating on the vehicles I've been fixing has been hard. Thankfully, I haven't had any big jobs assigned to me today, just a few tyres and oil changes, both I can do with my eyes shut.

I've done nothing but think about Ruby's words all day long. *"I like you too!"*

My wolf isn't letting me forget them either. He doesn't seem to care about all the reasons Ruby and me wouldn't work. The fact that our alpha would never allow it is just a little obstacle we can easily jump over. He's clearly delusional.

My boss's voice pulls me away from my thoughts of Ruby for the tenth time today. "Ed, there's some Sheila asking for you at reception. Something about a bike service?"

"That'll be Bel," I say wiping my hands on a rag and making my way through to the reception.

Bel pulls me into a hug not caring about the grease and oil I'm covered in, going on her leathers. "Hey Ed," she says as I struggle to get away from her.

"I'm oily, I don't want to make a mess of your leathers."

She releases me and gives me a good once over. "No one seemed to know I was coming. I only saw you this morning, so I know I haven't got the wrong day. Why are you so distracted?" Her smile suddenly turns to a sad frown. "Oh…Ed, you're so…" Not bothering to finish her sentence pulls me into a hug once again.

"I'm fine."

"You do realise I can feel exactly how *fine* you are not?" Releasing me, she starts to play with the keys in her hand. My misery is no doubt rubbing off on her. I need to get my head off Ruby and into my work.

"Let me just pull this car out and you can ride her into my bay," I say pointing to the bike parked outside. With a nod, Bel leaves the reception and I make my way back to the car I was working on so I can clear up space for Bel's bike.

In a matter of minutes, the car is out in the carpark and Bel's bike is in its place in my bay. Bel leans against the workbench at the end of the bay as she watches me drain the oil. "So…I guess it's a woman?"

Chicks! If it were a guy sitting there, he'd just leave me to my misery. Chicks always have to meddle. She'll just keep digging if I don't answer. *Fuck!* I can't tell her I'm in love with her mate's little sister. "A woman I can't have. I'll get over it."

"Why?"

I change the filter and start to refill the oil before answering, trying to give myself time to think of how to answer without telling her everything. "People who are important to her don't think I'm good enough for her." It's the truth.

Jumping down from the bench, Bel stands with her hands on her hips and a fierce look on her face. "You may be a flirt, but there's no one you aren't good enough for. Who are they? I'll tell them."

If only she knew she was mated to him.

"I appreciate the offer, Bel, but I'm not sure he'll take your word for it." I laugh.

"Aha, he? Is he an overprotective father?"

He sure acts like one.

"Yeah, although she has a few siblings who would probably feel the same. Honestly, I'll be okay. She'll probably hook up with someone and I'll move on."

"Or you'll want to tear him apart for touching your woman," she says with a frown. After the way I pinned Paddy to the car when I saw him kissing Ruby last night, I'm pretty sure she's onto something there.

Unable to deny it, I turn back to the bike without replying and carry on with the service. It doesn't take me long to swap out the spark plugs and have her fired up and growling nicely. I turn back to Bel and wave to the bike. "She's all yours, beautiful, it's not too late to ride off into the sunset with me," I flirt with a grin.

"I've got a couple of hours until sunset, I better go pack a bag," she says, playing along before throwing her arms around my neck and hugging me, without a care for the oil all over me. "Fine, I'll drop the subject, but if you don't get over her, I'm getting involved. Remember you can't fool me, Ed. I'm your alpha female and I'll make sure you're happy," she says while squeezing the breath out of me. She's almost out the doors before she comes shooting back in. "I almost forgot, Theo needs you to pop in tonight, he's got a job for you tomorrow."

I nod in acknowledgement and she drives off, probably heading home to her mate.

9. TAKE ONE FOR THE TEAM
Ruby

I walk into the kitchen expecting to find Selena and Chloe waiting for me, for our weekly visit to the day spa. I'm surprised to find Theo and Eddie chatting over coffee instead.

"Morning Rubes, you're head feeling any better today?" Eddie greets me as he takes a mouthful of his coffee.

I groan, embarrassed by the reminder of my idiocy from the night out. "Ed, did you have to remind me? I'd happily forgotten about my stupidity."

"You're not one of us until you've had a good ribbing about a bad night out," he laughs.

Knowing that no matter what he says, I'll never be one of them, I glance at my watch and quickly change the subject. "Where's Selena and Chloe?" I ask looking at Theo for an answer. If they aren't here, he'll know exactly where they are. He knows where everyone is.

Theo walks over to the sink and rinses out his cup. "Selena has an ultrasound appointment, Mum and Chloe went with her. Ed can go with you to your appointment at the spa," he announces nonchalantly, bending to place his cup in the dishwasher.

As annoyed as I am at the fact that Selena didn't even think to invite me along to her ultrasound, I can't hold back the laugh at the thought of how out of place Ed will look at the day spa.

"I'm not participating, I'm on bodyguard duty," Ed's voice full of authority making the words I was about to say die on my tongue.

I'd love to talk him into getting a pedicure or even better, a wax. That will be my mission for the day. I'm not leaving the spa until I've put Ed through something uncomfortable, it can be payback for the ribbing he mentioned earlier.

***

We drive in comfortable silence until we pull into the day spa's carpark.

"How are things with your mum, have you had a chance to chat some more?" Ed asks.

"I'm trying to give her a chance. She's seeing a therapist, and Theo says she isn't lying about her intentions. So I need to give her an opportunity at least to prove herself," I reply, feeling somewhat guilty because I can't just look past her previous indiscretions and give her the future she obviously wants.

He pulls into a parking space, removes the keys from the ignition and turns to look me in the eyes. "That's good. Trying is all you can do. If it doesn't work, it doesn't work. Sometimes your past can't be overlooked. You might come to forgive her in time, but unfortunately it's harder to forget."

Relief floods me, knowing that someone not only understands my side of things, but he doesn't expect me to forgive and forget. "Thanks Ed. You're the first person that hasn't expected me and Mum to be besties in a couple of months' time. You're pretty wise for a player."

A smile spreads across his face before he tries to wipe it off, and replace it with a look of horror. "Don't tell anyone, it will ruin my player reputation."

Reaching across the car and slapping his arm, I laugh. "As if anything could ruin that reputation of yours." I start to sing the Britney Spears song *'Womanizer'* as I exit the car and close the door behind me.

I don't get far before Eddie grabs me and starts to tickle my sides as I squeal and try to squirm away with no luck.

"Are you going to stop teasing me with that song? Or should I keep on tickling?" he asks while still prodding away at my ribs.

I can't take any more. "Yes," I shout between fits of laughter. "I'll...stop," I add.

His hands ease up on the tickles, but still grip my sides to hold me steady as I take a moment to catch my breath.

"Okay?" he queries, slowly releasing me. It's at that moment, I notice how close we actually are. I shiver at the loss of his body heat, even though it's a beautiful summer's day at thirty degrees Celsius.

"Yes," I say distractedly as I head for the entrance humming the tune to *'Womanizer.'*

"Ruby," Eddie growls low in his throat, a sexy sound that's sending butterflies through my stomach. But it's too late for him to punish me for it, now that I'm already pulling the door open. To tease him more and to show him I know I've gotten away with it, I poke my tongue out at him over my shoulder as I make my way to the receptionist.

"Later, Rubes. Just you wait," he threatens playfully.

"Hi. Ruby Wilson. I have a waxing appointment with Gloria," I say to the woman behind the counter.

"Go straight through, Ms. Wilson. Your friend can take a seat out here," she informs us with a pointed look at Eddie over my shoulder.

I nod, accepting her instructions until I feel Ed bristle behind me. "I'm going in with her," he demands leaving no room for argument.

It doesn't stop her. "I'm sorry, sir, but only paying customers can go back there, for health and safety reasons. If you would like to get a wax, you're more than welcome to join her," the woman announces smugly, confident he won't take her up on the offer.

"Are you good with your hands?" he asks the big flirt. Having seen her blush, he quickly adds, "How about a massage?" in a suggestive tone.

I watch as she gulps, opens her mouth to speak, and closes it again without saying another word. With one sentence, he's rendered her speechless.

I quietly hum the tune to *'Womanizer'* again as I turn my back to them both so I can hide the grin on my face. I feel his eyes trying to burn a hole in my back, but I don't stop humming.

"I'd be happy to offer you a…" She gulps once again. "A massage, but that's a waxing suite, so you'd need to book a wax," she informs him, making it clear that she'd happily give him more than a massage.

"Ed, looks like you'll have to man up and take one for the team," I tease.

"Fine. Book me in," he grumbles.

The woman behind the counter looks at Ed nervously, it's as if she wants to say something but daren't. Finally plucking up the courage she asks her question, "What kind of wax would you like? Back, chest or crack and sack?"

The look on Ed's face, a picture, as he mouths the words *'crack and sack'* in disbelief.

Remembering the sprinkling of chest hair I'd seen when he was only wearing a towel the other day, I decide to save him from any more trauma. "He'll take the chest wax," I say with finality, as I pull him into the waxing suite.

Closing the door behind us and knowing how these things work, I prepare myself for Gloria's entrance by promptly dropping my jeans to the floor and jumping up on the table.

Ed clears his throat. "Rubes, you can't just drop your jeans in front of me," he says sounding somewhat put out.

"Just be thankful I'm only getting my legs waxed. You'd be seeing a hell of a lot more, if it was time for my Brazilian," I say, only half-joking because I'm booked in for that in a fortnight.

Saving me from any smart remark he was thinking of embarrassing me with, Gloria, my beauty therapist, walks in silencing us both with her greeting. "Hello. I hear we have a new client today. I'll be gentle, I promise." The flirty tone coming from the grandmotherly looking woman before me stuns me for a minute before I realise Ed has been surprisingly quiet since my Brazilian remark.

With a glance over at Ed, I see the hungry look on his face as he's watching me intently. So much so, I don't know if he's even noticed Gloria's entrance or greeting.

"Morning, Gloria. Eddie here is a little nervous." My words seem to snap Eddie out of his trance, but he doesn't get to speak before Gloria jumps straight into business. "Since you're ready and in the hot seat, I guess you've decided to go first."

I hadn't really thought about going first, I was just in routine mode. I usually come in alone, not that I'll be admitting that to anyone. Theo would not be happy with Chloe for dropping her duty so she could have a massage. Playing along with Gloria's suggestion, I quickly agree. "Yes, I figured this way Eddie can see that there's nothing to it."

"Eddie, there's a seat by the wall over there." She distractedly points over her shoulder in the direction of the chair as she gathers the things she'll need to do the procedure. "Sit back and relax for a few minutes." It sounded more like an order, even to my human ears.

Not making a move to follow her instructions he steps closer to my side, making sure to be out of her way. "I can see better over here," is all he says.

It doesn't take Gloria long to do my legs, I'm quickly jumping down and pulling my jeans on. Gloria turns her attention to Eddie. "If you just take your shirt off and lie down, we can get started and it will be over in no time."

"You just want to see the goods under the shirt," he declares with a grin. I'm seriously starting to worry that he doesn't know how to communicate without flirting when it comes to the female species.

"Behave," Gloria chides, as he pulls his shirt over his head and does as he's told laying on the table.

The sight of his washboard abs throws me as I fumble with the button on my jeans. I wouldn't mind being Gloria right now, getting paid to touch his chest. I quickly gather myself and pull my tongue back in my mouth before making my way to stand next to Eddie as he had me earlier. "Ready for the pain, Eddie?" I tease.

"It didn't look too bad when she did your legs," he says confidently.

Gloria smears some warm wax onto his chest covering the sprinkling of hair, placing a strip over it, she counts down from three. "Three, two…" Ripping it off before she even gets to one.

"Fuck!" Ed shouts, taking a breath as though he'd held it. "Holy shit, do I have any skin left?" he asks as he lifts his head, looking down at the pink patch of skin on his chest.

Gloria doesn't bat an eyelid before she smears on more wax and places another strip over it. She doesn't bother with the countdown this time. She just rips it off.

Eddie manages to control himself, this time only giving a grunt of pain. "Where was my countdown?" his voice sounding strained.

"I thought it would be best to just get on with it," she proclaims, matter-of-fact. All the while loading his chest with more wax and strips before ripping them off one by one.

She made quick work of it. After ripping off the last strip and ensuring she had all the hairs, I watch as she grabs an oiled up wipe and starts smoothing it over his chest removing any remaining wax residue. My hands are itching to take over and rub their way all over that oiled up chest. I quickly fold my arms over my chest and trap my hands under my arms before they can follow through. Hanging around with these hot guys is sending me crazy. I've never fantasised over guys before, not even when I was surrounded by plenty of them back home. I'm here for a couple of months, and I'm having to physically trap my hands to stop from touching the guys. Maybe werewolves have stronger pheromones or something.

"Are you okay, Rubes?"

Eddie's voice pulls me out of my inner turmoil and I tear my eyes away from Gloria's hands on his chest. "Yeah. I can't wait to tell the other guys about this." I laugh.

"You're all done. If you want to get dressed and go see Donna at the front desk, she'll be happy to book you in for your next appointment," Gloria says as she wipes her hands off and leaves the room, closing door behind her. I'm suddenly aware of how small the room is and how close I'm standing to Eddie.

"You will not say a word of this to anyone," he demands. I take a step back giving him room to put his shirt on. "This shit stinks," he says pointing to his oiled up chest. "They'll smell me coming a mile away, but as far as anyone else is concerned I had a massage. Okay?"

"What do I get for keeping my mouth shut?" I enquire.

"Ruby," he says in a warning tone, as he pulls his shirt over his head.

"Telling everyone would be so much fun. Watching them ribbing you about it for weeks would be *very* entertaining," I tease. It would be fun, I can hear them laughing and jesting already.

He looks at me menacingly as he walks forward, the look in his eye causes me to back up until I'm against the door.

"You said plenty of entertaining things when you were drunk the other night, you spill the beans on this, and I'll have to share a few things myself," he says leaning into me. Panic flows through me, I thought I'd remembered everything I said the other night. Is he leaning into kiss me? Did I come onto him, when I was drunk? His hand reaches around my hip and he opens the door. I stumble back slightly as the door moves behind me and I slip through.

"Fine, my lips are forever sealed," I admit defeat, not knowing what secrets he could spill if I don't.

10. BBQs and Backyard Cricket
Ruby

Walking out into the yard, with a plateful of bread rolls I glance at the stack of sausages on the barbie and start to wonder if we're going to have anyone else turn up. We have enough food to feed the whole pack, but it's only close members, or who I call *family*, that Theo and Bel invited. The guys are all gathered around the barbie, Eddie, Paddy, Jared, Billy, Wes and Theo. I place the plate on the table and grab a beer from the Esky as I pass and head to the girls lounging on the grass. Mum pats the grass between her and Misty, inviting me to join her. Things are still strange between the two of us, I've been avoiding her at all costs, but unfortunately I can't do that today. I take the seat offered knowing it would only look vindictive if I tried to make a space between someone else.

"Thanks, Mum," I say grateful for the seat.

The guys all make their way over to the table.

"Food's ready, ladies," Theo announces as the guys all start making up their plates. "Before we eat, Bel and I have an announcement." Bel makes her way over to him and hugs into his side lovingly, as the rest of us all head for the table.

"When we mated it was a crazy time. We had The Controller running rampant and not to mention my ex-wife showing up out of the blue. So, we think it's about time we have our mating ceremony."

"Congratulations," Alyssa says pulling Bel into a hug. "How much time do we have to pull this wedding together?" she asks as she releases Bel.

"Congratulations, Ted, I'm so happy for you," I say giving my big brother a hug and calling him by his pet name. "Love you," I say as pull away and step back for Alyssa to grab him for a hug.

"Love you too, little sis," he says before turning his attention to Alyssa.

"Three months isn't much time, but I think we can work with that," she says. I must have missed Bel's answer when I was hugging Theo.

"Pups..." Theo says sounding stunned to match his wide eyes.

Alyssa having not seen his face wriggles free of his hold. "You never know what the future might bring, of course, you guys can try for pups." She giggles nervously.

"No." He's starting to sound crazy even to my ears and I know my brother pretty well, he's not looking far off it, either.

Bel strokes a hand down his forearm. "Babe?"

Ignoring his mate, Theo's eyes flit between Wes and Alyssa. "No, you're having pups," he says. The way his eyes are flitting between the two of them I can see he's here, in the moment, and not having some crazy episode. "Alyssa, you're pregnant."

Suddenly each and every werewolf inhales all at once, no doubt trying to scent the hormones or something. Mum and I, not knowing what else to do, look at each other and smile warily. It's somewhat comforting to know I'm not the only human around for once. I'm not alone with this feeling of being an outsider. Thinking back to my mum's reasoning for her turning to drugs, I can see how maybe her life with my father could have pushed her that way. Especially, after her sons had been ripped from her life. Looking at my mother now, I can imagine the strength it must have taken to not only face me and my brother but to become the outsider in a pack once again. She did it for us.

A round of congratulations for both couples flows through the yard.

"You need another alpha to officiate the ceremony. Who are you going to ask?" I hear Wes question Theo, as I start to fill my plate with food.

"Who do I trust? Is a better question. Jesse O'Keefe from the Rossi Pack in WA is the only alpha I've ever felt at ease with, but he's not been the same since his mate went missing five years ago. I don't know if he'd be willing to do it considering his circumstances."

Wes nods his understanding as he takes a bite of a burger.

"You'll never know if you don't ask," Bel says placing a kiss on his shoulder as she reaches past him for a bread roll on the table.

With my plate full, I look around the garden for somewhere to sit, spotting Paddy on lounger at the back. I head over deciding to bite the bullet and face the embarrassing things I did while I was drunk the other night. We've already discussed what happened when I first had the flashbacks, but I still feel sorry for throwing myself at him.

I grab an extra beer as I pass the Esky. Looking up at my arrival he gives me a sheepish smile.

"Peace offering," I say holding out the beer for him.

He takes the beer and places it at his feet next to his already half full bottle. "There's no need for that. Take a seat."

I shrug as I sit in the chair beside him. "I still feel bad about the other night." Not wanting to say something that makes me feel any stupider, I take a bite of my burger.

He reaches his hand out and places it on my arm halting me from taking my next bite. "Honestly, you didn't throw yourself at me. I wouldn't have danced with you if I didn't want something to happen."

I give a jerky nod, not knowing how else to reply. He removes his hand and starts back in on his food.

"Jared said you were doing an OUA course, what subject are you doing?"

I swallow a mouthful of beer and tell him all about my criminology course, probably too much. When I get talking about something I'm passionate about I struggle to stop. He sits quietly taking in every word I say, smiling at all the right moments.

"It sounds like something you actually enjoy," he says when I finally shut my mouth.

I grin at him and let the truth of my words show. "I love it."

"Do you want to join the police academy, when you finish?" he asks, lifting his drink to his lips and swallowing what's left in the bottle, before licking them clean. He catches my eye as he puts the bottle down.

I can't help but blush at being caught getting distracted by his lips, lips I've had the pleasure of feeling on my own. Not that I can really remember what they felt like. "Yeah, that's the plan. Hopefully with the degree behind me, I can fast track into the field I'm interested in. I'll still have to do the initial training and I'll probably have to do the first couple of years on the job like everyone else, but I know where I essentially want to be in the end." I suddenly realise I don't know what he does. "What do you do?" I query.

"I'm doing a graphic design course, I only have this semester left and then I'll be let loose on the world. Well, that's if someone will give me a job."

"Doesn't anyone want to give you a go?"

"It turns out that everyone wants to design websites and things these days. Theo asked me to design him a website for his carving business, and he said he was going to chat to the other alpha's about setting up a communication network so all the packs can stay in contact better. So the degree won't be entirely useless. I just might have to look at other jobs in the long run."

"Oh, that network thing is a great idea. Theo was only talking about another alpha having a missing mate. I'm sure if there was a network set up we could spread her picture further and she might be found."

"Oh yes, Jesse. I don't know how he still goes on without Frankie, not knowing where she is." He shakes his head. "I've never experienced the mating bond myself, but I know it's strong. I don't think I'd be able to handle not knowing where she is or what's happened to her."

"Going by how Wes reacted when Alyssa was taken by The Controller, I can only imagine the strength Jesse must have, to have not lost control of his wolf or pack," I say honestly stunned at the thought.

"Are you two up for some backyard cricket? Girls versus boys," Bel asks as she passes by heading to the shed, no doubt to dig out the cricket set.

With a shrug, we both get up and follow her as she makes her way to the middle of the yard, cricket set in hand. "Girls bat first," she says handing me the bat.

I take the bat and give it a wary look. "You've never seen me play cricket before have you, Bel? Maybe I shouldn't bat." I'm the worst cricket player, last time I played Theo banned me from ever playing again. I've got a habit of throwing the bat like in softball or baseball. If I wasn't playing with werewolves, I would have probably hospitalised half the fielders.

"Ruby's banned from backyard cricket," Theo orders. The other pack members nod their agreement, leaving Mum and Bel looking at me with caution.

"She can't be that bad," Bel declares, sticking up for me. Unfortunately, she's very wrong.

"I am," I admit unabashedly.

"Well, I don't care. It's a family game and we're all playing," Bel demands, setting up the stumps behind me.

"You'll regret that decision later, baby," Theo mutters as he takes the ball and swings his arm to stretch ready for bowling.

Once everyone is in position Theo bowls the first ball. I'm expecting the ball to connect with the wickets behind me, but to my surprise it's the bat that connects with the ball. My internal chant of *'don't drop the bat, don't drop the bat,'* helps me manage to keep a hold of the bat as I run to the safety of the stick where Theo bowled from. Bel runs from that side and stops where I'd started. I hadn't hit the ball hard enough to get any more than the one run.

"Get ready for a good run, Rubes," Bel says as she positions herself for Theo's bowl. I do as I'm told and brace myself to run and run hard. I don't even see the ball go past, the thunderous whack it makes when it connects with the bat is my starting gun. I bolt to the stumps and back, Bel waves me on so I run again. I feel the ball brush past me as I hit the floor at the base of the stumps with my bat. Calling my safety. It hits the wickets a second later and the guys all groan at the near miss.

I manage to hit the next ball Theo throws, and I hit it hard enough to do a double run. I stand ready for the next bowl, it sails right past the bat and hits the wicket behind me. The guys cheer and I hand the bat to Delly, a pack member who I would guess is around my age.

"Okay guys, the real game starts now," she says, insinuating that they were only pretending to play while I was batting. Fucking bitch, just wait until we're fielding, she'll be getting a ball to the back of her head once or twice, I'm certain of that.

I head over to the other girls waiting out at the edge of the yard to bat. "You did well to hit anything Theo threw your way," Paddy compliments me as I pass him in the field.

"Thanks," I blush, knowing he's only being kind. I know they were all holding back while I was playing, but there was no need for Delly to make me feel so inferior. I sit down realising too late who I've sat next to. "Mum," I greet her with a smile.

"Ignore the bitch, she's only jealous because that cutie has his eye on you," Mum announces, nodding toward Paddy. I follow her nod with my eyes and catch the glare Delly throws my way. *Just great!*

"Mum, did you forget she's got werewolf hearing?" I question. Knowing everyone on the field just heard her comment.

"No, I wanted the bitch to hear," she claims, the few snickers in the field make me grin. I lean in and give my mum a side hug.

"Thanks, Mum," I whisper. Maybe we can fix things between us after all.

***

The girls won by five runs. So bragging rights are ours until the next game, which is amazing because I'm pretty sure the girls have never won before. Bel is like a pro, she says she hasn't actually played before, but I'm sure she's telling porky's, I'll be grilling Jared later.

The doorbell rings through the house.

"That'll be the pizza," Bel shouts into the house from out back. Bel and Alyssa are still clearing the table from earlier.

"I'll get the door, Eddie, get everyone's money together," Jared announces heading for the door.

"You heard the man, guys, give me your money. Girls, you better enjoy this, because you won't win again," Eddie proclaims as the guys dig into their pockets with muttered complaints about letting us win. After collecting all the money he heads through to the front door, it's only a few seconds later when both Jared and Eddie enter loaded up with pizza boxes. I hear Eddie call my name out, but rather than fight through the hungry wolves I wait back until everyone gets their pizzas.

Paddy barges through the crowd with two boxes in hand. "Here, I thought I'd save you the fight."

I take the box he offers. "Thanks!" The smell that hits me when opening it is mouth-watering. I love Hawaiian pizzas, pineapple and ham. Yum.

"Pineapple? Oh, I don't think we can be friends anymore," he says looking disturbed at my choice of pizza topping.

"That means you won't be stealing my leftovers like Eddie and Jared usually do. You can come more often," I say before taking a huge bite out of the first slice.

"Your pizza is safe with me," he laughs, before tucking into his own.

I manage to eat three slices before I'm well and truly stuffed. "Okay, I'm done, who wants it?" I ask holding the closed box up. It practically flies out my hand as Jared takes it with a cheer. Eddie stops before me a second later.

"I thought you loved me, Ruby. I'm pack, you should have saved it for me. Not given it to the intruder," Eddie says glumly.

"Ha! You're too slow, Ed," Jared teases.

"She obviously has a new favourite. She's just teasing you all, she'll never put out," Delly insists her voice snarky, catching everyone's attention.

I stand, ready to go on the defensive.

"Delly!" Theo's warning tone shows he's clearly not happy with her. As much as I love my brother, she'll never respect me if I sit back and hide behind him.

I take a step in her direction. "You clearly have a problem with me, Delly, what is it?"

She glances at Theo as if she's seeking permission. "I've asked you the question, don't look at him. I want an answer. I'm not living with this tension between us. I want to know what's bothering you?"

With a huff, she lays it all out. "I've watched these guys paw all over you every summer and never battered an eyelid, knowing that once those eight weeks are over you'll be heading home and the females of the pack will get the attention back. I'm not being a bitch, these guys," she says waving an arm around the room blindly, "they're the future of the pack. We've all been brought up together, some of us will wait for our true mates, and others will choose a pack member to mate with. Every time you come home and flirt with them you're taking the chance of a mate away from one of the females. Now you live here for good, it's not going to stop unless you date one of them. At least that way the others can focus their attention elsewhere." She looks at me with pleading eyes.

"Thank you, for being honest. But it's been known for werewolves to mate with humans too. Hell, I came from one of those matings. In saying that, I don't think the guys give me any more attention than they do any other female, but I'll be more aware for future interaction," I say as I turn and leave the room. I was being honest, I don't think the guys focus on me when I'm home. Not unless Theo has set them on guard duty, it's not like we hang out in our free time except for in family get-togethers like today. The boys night out, the other night was a one off and after the state I was in, I don't think that will be happening again anytime soon. Deciding I've had enough I head to my room. Reaching out, I turn the door handle as I reach my room when a hand on my shoulder spins me around.

I find myself face to face with Paddy. "Don't let her chase you away, Ruby. Did you mean what you said about mating? Would that be something you'd be interested in, if you met the right wolf, of course?"

I swallow the lump in my throat and nod. "The pack is part of my life. You know how overprotective my brothers are, would you expect them to be happy if I married a human? I'm pretty sure they would want me protected by a werewolf mate."

Paddy nods with a smirk. "Yeah, I think you're onto something there. They aren't the only ones that wouldn't be happy with you marrying a human."

I move to turn toward my room. "I'm not letting Delly chase me away. It's late, so I'm going to call it a night."

His hand that's still resting on my shoulder halts me from turning. "Before you go, do you fancy going out somewhere with me tomorrow?"

"What, like a date?" I ask, feeling my cheeks blush. Jesus, if I can't handle him asking me out, how am I meant to handle a freaking date?

"Yeah, exactly like a date," he says throwing me a wink.

"I'd love to," I answer honestly. I've had a thing for Paddy for a while now. He's a nice guy, not to mention gorgeous, what eighteen-year-old girl wouldn't have a thing for him? It would be stupid to say no.

"Great, can you be ready for ten in the morning? We can make a day of it," he says with an uncertain smile on his face as though he's worried that I'd say no.

"I think I can manage that," I tease, with a wry grin, as I back away from him.

"See you tomorrow then," he says as he turns and heads back downstairs. I stand with my hand on the door handle at my back, watching him make his way down the stairs, so I catch him as he turns to get one last look.

"Night," he says somewhat shyly.

I can't wipe the huge grin off my face even as I close myself in my bedroom.

11. CONFESSIONS OF A FIRST DATE
Ruby

I head downstairs to warn Theo that Paddy will be picking me up for a date soon. I don't know if he'll be pissed that I'm dating a pack member, or if my guess the night before about him wanting me under a wolf's protection over a human's, would work in our favour. To be honest, I'm pretty sure he isn't ready for his little sister to be dating anyone.

I knock on his office door knowing he'll be there checking through his emails, with his morning coffee like he is at that time every day.

"Come on in, Rubes," he calls from behind the closed door. I know not to stress on how he knew it was me, I've been around the wolves long enough to know that they have this strange sixth sense when it comes to someone being behind a closed door. Scent, the psychic bond that belongs to the wolves, which Theo insists I am part of, and even the sound of your knock are all tells.

I open the door and make my way to his side as he peers at the laptop screen before him, planting a kiss on his cheek I give him a side hug before clearing a space on the edge of his desk and planting my butt on it.

Lifting his eyes from the screen he focuses his attention on me as he sits back in his seat. "You went to bed pretty early last night, is everything okay?"

"Yeah, I'm fine. I'd just had enough and thought an early night was a good idea," I reply somewhat honestly. The look in his eye's telling me he can see there's more to it and he's right, but I don't want to go into it. I break the eye contact by glancing around the room to find anything I can use to distract him.

"I hope you didn't take anything Delly said to heart, she was out of order and I've spoken to her about it. You're pack, and she needs to treat you as she would any other female pack member. If she isn't willing to try and tear a guy's attention from you, she doesn't deserve that guy as a mate. It's as simple as that," he says, apparently not willing to drop the subject.

I look up quickly so I can see his face. Did he really mean that? Was he really okay with me being a pack member and dating as one?

I ask him, "Do you really mean that? You'd be happy with me dating a pack member, maybe eventually mating with one?"

"Let's get something straight, I won't be happy with you dating anyone, ever. But I know I'm going to have to deal with it eventually unless you have any interest in joining a convent. Have you ever been interested in becoming a nun? You did love that movie as a kid, you know, the one with the woman who makes dresses out of some ugly arse curtains?" We both laugh before he carries on, "Seriously, though, I'll hate it but I'll deal with it. The only consolation I get with it being a pack member is I'll know if he can protect you or not."

I guess now is as good as any to test that theory. "It's good that you feel that way because Paddy will be picking me up in a minute." I watch as a number of emotions play over his face before he speaks.

"He did mention something about that last night."

"He asked for your permission?" The thought actually pisses me off.

"No, he was telling me not asking. It was after he'd followed you upstairs." He sounds angry at that thought, which makes me somewhat happy. "Although I'm a little concerned because I thought it was Ed that you liked. I'm not complaining, I'm far happier that it's Paddy you're interested in. He's better suited to you," he adds. Making me lose the happy feeling I just had.

"You can like more than one person, Theo. I'd never have a chance with Eddie, he's completely out of my league. Paddy likes me back and has asked me out, so my interest in Paddy has taken over my interest in Eddie," I try to explain.

Why the hell am I babbling? I'm sure he's had crushes in his time.

"As long as he treats you right and keeps you happy, I won't interfere."

Jumping off the desk I pounce on my brother, engulfing him in a hug. "Thanks. I love you, Ted." My pet name for him sneaking out once again.

Hearing the doorbell ring he pushes me off him. "Go have fun."

"I will," I say as I run to the door. I don't need my mum answering and letting him in, if she finds out what's happening she'll give him the fifth degree now and me it later.

"And for God's sake, behave," I hear Theo shout as I run through the house.

Stopping in front of the door, I quickly straighten my clothes and check that I look presentable in the mirror on the wall, silently thanking my brother for being vain enough to need a mirror in the entry hall. Thinking on it, it was probably something Selena insisted on, back when they were married. Shaking the stupid thoughts out of my head, I pull the door open and greet Paddy with a smile.

"These are for you," he says pushing a bunch of sunflowers into my hands.

"Thanks, I...How did you know they were my favourites?" I ask, flicking a look down at the flowers.

"I do pay attention, you know. I've seen the little sunflower tattoo you have."

I swallow nervously, wondering when he's seen that tattoo, it's extremely low on my hip I didn't know anyone knew about it. I quickly manage to compose myself.

"Come in a minute, I'll put these in water and grab my purse." I turn and go straight to the kitchen, the sound of the door closing and heavy footsteps tells me Paddy is following behind.

I pause in the doorway, spotting Mum using the coffee machine. Taking a deep breath I prepare myself for the Spanish Inquisition.

"Morning, sweetheart. Nice to see you again, Paddy," Mum says. "Let me put them in water," she adds clocking the flowers. "You two get going. Have fun."

Surprised by her offer I stay silent.

"Thanks, Mrs. Wilson," Paddy says, taking the flowers from my grasp and passing them to Mum.

"Please, call me, Trudy," she says as she digs a vase out of the first cupboard she looks in. How did she know it was there? I've lived here for months at a time over the years and I had no idea if Theo even owned a vase?

"Ruby?" Paddy's voice pulls me out of my head.

I quickly give Mum an appreciative hug. "Thanks, Mum." Taking Paddy's outstretched hand, I drag him toward the door. Snatching my purse and phone off the kitchen bench as we pass.

Once buckled in the car and moving down the drive, I turn to Paddy. "So, where are we going?"

"It's a surprise, but Theo assured me you'll like it," he says as he takes his eyes off the road to throw me a wink.

"You tease! Stop winking and get your eyes back on the road."

As we pull onto the freeway, I have a guess at where we are heading. "Are we going to Sydney?"

"Yes, Miss Marple, we are going to Sydney. Choose some music and stop trying to guess things," he says passing me his phone. I flick through his playlists and select the James Bay album I've been meaning to buy.

The album ends just as we enter the city. On driving through, I give up trying to guess where he's taking me, I sit back and enjoy his company. He tells me about his family who he hasn't seen for the last six years, not since the day he was attacked by a werewolf. The pack the werewolf belonged to was brutal. They didn't think they could do anything with a thirteen-year-old, newly changed pup, they'd planned to kill him, but luckily one of the females in the pack had a connection to Theo. She managed to get Paddy to Theo before they executed him. I had no idea where Paddy had come from, I remember one summer I turned up and there was a new wolf.

Theo spoke to his parents, he told them it wasn't safe for Paddy to live with them until he had a handle on his wolf. The wolves are secretive, but I guess when someone is attacked they can't just leave the family in the dark especially when it's a child that's been changed.

Paddy tells me how he was the baby of the family, his sisters being eight and ten years older than him.

"I miss them. They probably have kids of their own now," he admits, the sadness in his voice evident.

"Have you ever thought of going back? You aren't a danger to them anymore," I ask. I don't think I'd ever be able to stay away from my family. I can't imagine being so dangerous you have to be taken away, your life changed forever.

"I still have moments when my wolf doesn't listen. You heard about how I almost attacked Bel a few months back?" he questions. He pulls the car into a car park. Taking in my surroundings I realise we are at the ice rink. Finding a space near the entry he pulls in and stops the car.

"Bel's blood is different, even Theo had a moment, and it was a full moon. You've never attacked me and how many times have I bled in front of you over the years?"

"Yeah, you are pretty clumsy. You have a good point. Anyway, let's forget about all that. We're meant to be having fun," he says getting out the car.

Taking my hand, he walks me to the entrance of the ice rink.

"We're skating," I say stating the obvious. "I haven't been here in years. Theo used to bring me when he wasn't busy with pack stuff."

"He brought me once or twice when you weren't home. I'm pretty sure he had a thing for the chick in the café," he laughs.

"He was madly in love with Selena," I remind him.

"Okay, I think his wolf had a thing for the chick that worked in the café," he clarifies.

"Theo is the first to admit that his wolf wasn't a big fan of Selena, but he'd never have cheated on her." I can't help but defend my brother, he was an idiot for many things he did in regards to Selena and their relationship - like not telling her he was a wolf. He still hasn't told her and she's living with a number of them under his roof. But he isn't a cheater.

"I didn't say he cheated, he just liked to look," Paddy says giving my hand a little squeeze. "Come on, let's get some skates so we can have a race."

"What's the prize?" I ask hoping he can see the fun we could have with this.

He pays the man behind the counter our admission fee. "Winners choice," he says with a smirk as he looks at me.

Pulling my hand out of his, I run for the skate stand. "Be prepared to lose," I throw over my shoulder.

"Oh, those right there are fighting words, Miss Wilson."

12. BARBARIANS AND DRAGONS
Paddy

As I walk Ruby to her front door, I start to worry about whether any of my fellow pack members might be spying on us. The fact that there are no cars parked in the drive eases my concerns but only slightly.

"Thanks for today, I've had the best day," Ruby says as she turns from the door to face me.

"Thank you for taking me up on the offer." A piece of her hair falls across her face and I can't help myself from reaching out and tucking it behind her ear. She leans into my hand welcoming the contact, making my wolf sit up and take notice. "You still haven't claimed your prize yet," I say remembering her beating me at the rink.

Bloody hockey skates, how was I supposed to know they helped with speed?

She grins up at me mischievously as she lifts a hand and runs her fingers along my jaw. My wolf wants me to beg for more of that touch.

"I think I'll save it for a rainy day."

"You're a little minx," I laugh and decide to bite the bullet and lean in for a kiss.

Our lips touch and she doesn't push me away. Her lips part slightly offering me access and I take it. I kiss her, showing everything I feel, everything I've felt for her for a while now. Her little moan of appreciation almost does me in. I push my wolf back reminding him we can't take her, not on our first date. Thankfully he listens, not wanting to scare her away he allows me to end the kiss.

Releasing the grip she has on my shirt, Ruby takes a small step back and looks up at me with unfocused eyes. She's the most beautiful woman I've ever laid eyes on. An angel. *Our angel,* my wolf growls appreciatively.

"I best get going, if I kiss you again, Theo will have my head," I say nodding toward the twitching blinds in the window beside us.

"He wouldn't dare..." she threatens, probably knowing if he was spying he'd be able to hear her with his wolf's hearing. The glint in her eye screams trouble. "Fine," she says grabbing my shirt front in her fists and pulling me against her again. I barely have time to steady myself with my hands on her hips, before she takes my mouth with hers. She releases my shirt and runs her hands up my chest and around the back of my neck, playing with the tips of my hair through her fingers. I dig my fingers into her hips, reminding myself too late she's only human and will bruise if I'm not careful.

The door behind Ruby bursts open and she's suddenly pulled from my grasp. "That's enough. She'll call you tomorrow," Theo says with finality, before slamming the door in my face. Knowing what he says goes, I head back to my car. Grinning at the protesting I can hear coming from Ruby.

I'm just pulling into my street as I hear my phone chime, alerting me that I have a text message. I pull into the drive and park behind Ed's Ford XR8 ute before digging my phone from my jean's pocket to check the message.

Ruby: My brother is a barbarian. D=

Another message comes through before I have a chance to reply.

Ruby: I had a fab day, thank U. X

I quickly type out my reply as I unlock the front door.

Me: Just remember he could be worse. I had a great day too. So thank U. ;)

"About fucking time. It's Game of Thrones night. What kept you out so late?" Ed shouts from the lounge.

In two minds about what to tell him, I delay by heading to the fridge for a beer first. "I'm grabbing a beer, do you want one?" I know he'll find out about my date sooner or later, but I have an inkling that he has his own feelings for Ruby. Not that he'll admit it. I've hung back for so long waiting for him to make a move on her but he hasn't. We're guys, we don't talk about feelings and shit, but at a guess, he thinks he's not worthy of her, which is stupid because if any guy is good enough for Ruby, it's him. He's as tough as nails, so he'd protect her fiercely, and he has a heart of gold that he'd worship her with. I'm not sure how he'll react to the details. He's my best mate and as much as he'll want to be happy for me, I think he'll be far from it.

"Okay, you're late in for Game of Thrones night and you *ask* me if I want a beer, something's definitely on your mind."

Grabbing two bottles, I close the fridge and sit on the other end of the sofa. I crack both bottles open and pass one across to Ed.

"Come on, tell Uncle Ed all about it," he jokes, before taking a sip of beer.

"Fucker!" Laughing I punch him in the arm playfully, making him choke on the beer. "I was on a date–"

"And you didn't tell me about it beforehand," he interrupts playfully holding a hand to his heart. "I'm wounded."

"A date with Ruby."

The smile drops off his face instantly, but he doesn't speak straightaway. I open my mouth to say something, anything, when he breaks his silence.

"Good, you both deserve to be loved up with someone." He doesn't sound even a bit convincing. I brace myself waiting for his rage, but instead he presses play on the remote. "We better not make the Mother of Dragons wait any longer," he adds effectively ending the conversation.

13. SCARRED FOR LIFE
Ruby

Paddy and I have been dating for almost a month now. I had offered to cook a meal for everyone, but Alyssa and Wes wanted a quiet night in. Mum has taken the pregnant Selena under her wing and is having a girl's night at Chloe's apartment. Theo, Bel, Jared, Eddie, Paddy and myself managed to sit through a whole meal without too much tension. Eddie has been off with me for a while now, I don't know what I've done to piss him off, but it's got to be something because he's fine with everyone else. Paddy insists that I should just leave him be, but I miss him. I miss the Eddie that had become a close friend. I leave the table clearing all the plates into the dishwasher.

"Let's stick a movie in," Bel announces dragging Theo into the lounge room.

I close the dishwasher, switch it on and move to follow Bel and Theo. Holding me back, Paddy pulls me into his warm embrace.

"The meal was lovely, angel, you did good," he says before kissing me senseless. My heart would be a flutter at the term of endearment if the kiss weren't sending it into overdrive. Our lips part and once I have enough sense to breathe again, I register Eddie talking behind us.

"I need a fucking drink!" he snaps pushing past us and heading for the front door. He's been strange with me lately, long gone is the caring Eddie who nursed me through my drunken state. I step away from Paddy ready to go after him and find out what the hell is going on when Jared places a hand on my shoulder to hold me back.

"I'll go. Wait up, Ed, I could do with a good drink myself," he shouts as he follows in Ed's wake.

"What's his problem?" I grumble, not really expecting an answer. He's ruined the good feeling I had from Paddy's kiss.

Lifting my chin with a finger, Paddy gently presses his lips against mine before pulling back millimetres. "Stop worrying and kiss me!" he demands before taking my lips once again.

Who am I to argue with a demand like that?

"Are you going to kiss all night or are you going to watch this movie?" Bel shouts from the lounge. *Movie or kiss?* We both pull away with a groan and head for the lounge.

"We chose *'Expendables 3'*," Bel reports as we take a seat on the sofa. With Bel and Theo cuddled up on the other sofa, it's a good job Eddie and Jared left, they would've looked funny cuddled up on the smaller two seater sofa. Bel doesn't wait for us to get comfortable before she presses play.

***

The movie finishes in no time. Hearing an intimate giggle I glance over in my brother's direction, regretting it the instant my eyes land on the loved up couple with their hands happily roaming over each other's body, not caring that they aren't alone.

"Do you *have* to do that so publicly?" I complain, half-heartedly. You can't be too begrudging, not when you see how much they love each other.

"She's right, let's go to bed," Bel suggests.

Theo groans without moving. "I'm comfy here."

"We could be naked and comfortable in bed," Bel says with a knowing smirk. Another visual I didn't need. Living with my brother is going to scar me for life.

"Well, if you put it that way," he says, as he gets up and throws Bel, who lets out a squeal, over his shoulder.

Both Paddy and I watch them leave, once they're out of sight and I can no longer hear them, Paddy turns to me with a smile. "I love seeing them like that."

Surprised by his comment, I joke, "Whatever floats your boat."

"No," he laughs. "It makes me look forward to being mated one day. Hopefully soon." I would say the look that crosses his face is almost a shy one.

I glance back at the door my brother and Bel had both left through and smile. "Me too," I say absently. To have that bond, that connection with someone, must be incredible. For a second, I hope that Paddy is thinking about us when he imagines himself with his mate because I am.

14. THE ONE
Paddy

The look on Ruby's face, as she looks in the direction the loved-up couple went, gives me the confidence to throw a corny line at her. "Do you know, that sexy dress of yours will look fantastic on my bedroom floor?"

She swallows nervously. "Well, we might just have to test that theory out," she says playfully. The way she's blinking up at me all innocently, I can't help but pull her into my lap and kiss her deeply. She breaks the kiss and catches her breath. "What did I do to deserve that?"

"Nothing, since when do I need a reason to kiss the woman I love?" I ask back. The shock on her face makes me go over my words again. I just told her I love her.

She recovers her composure quickly. "When you put it that way, you don't need one." Leaning into me she gives me a quick peck on the lips before jumping up and grabbing my hand. "Come on then, you better drive quickly because I need to show you how much I love you, and I can't do that with my brother and his freaky wolf hearing under the same roof." My wolf perks up at the admission. Grateful that she thought of her brother's hearing, I allow her to pull me up and lead me to the car.

The drive over to mine is a quiet one, it's a comfortable silence, though. I use the time to tell my wolf to hang back and allow Ruby to take the lead. We've refrained from being intimate up until now for various reasons, one being that Ruby hasn't had good experiences with sex in the past. There's no way I want to pressure her into anything she isn't ready for. In the heat of the moment, she's pushed for more a few times, but I know from experience, in the heat of the moment you'll sometimes agree to things you'll regret later.

We pull up on the drive and Ruby gives a little gasp at the sight of Ed's ute parked before us.

"He's out for the night. You saw the mood he was in, he probably won't be back until the early hours of the morning," I reassure her.

"Sorry, I just panicked because of his hearing and everything," she explains.

We exit the car and I let us in the house. I barely have the door closed before she jumps into my arms, wrapping her legs around my waist and her arms around my neck, before kissing me thoroughly. I stride through the house blindly, until we stumble into my bedroom. I break the heated kiss, placing her gently on the bed. She looks up at me with her dilated eyes and swollen lips.

"You're beautiful," I tell her as I take a step back. I'm barely holding onto my wolf. He's never wanted someone so much before. *We can't claim her, not our first time,* I remind him. He throws himself at me in anger. I take another step back. "Are you sure you want this, Ruby? We can wait," I assure her.

She stands, and walks toward me with slow, sure steps. "I'm sure. I'm not a virgin, but my past experiences haven't exactly been consensual, I'm ready for it to be. And you're the one I want my first time to be with," she says, lifting her dress over her head. "Now get naked so I can show you how ready I am."

Her nakedness, the smell of her arousal and her words ruin my resolve. I strip before she gets within touching distance, shredding my clothes from my body.

She bites her lip as her eyes roam my body hungrily.

Not able to keep my hands off her any longer, I pull her into my arms and pin her beneath me on the bed, ready to show her how good sex can be, when it's with someone who loves you.

15. FROM HEAVEN TO HELL IN A SECOND
Paddy

Feeling a small body snuggle into me wakes me from my slumber. I glance down at Ruby as she uses my arm as a pillow and I can't help but wonder how comfortable that could really be? I'm surprised to find I don't regret last night, not one bit. I'd been holding off on taking our relationship that step further because I wanted to make sure I was ready to take her as a mate. Looking at her now, I can't imagine waking up with anyone else again.

I watch as her green eyes pop open and she smiles up at me nervously. "Morning, beautiful," I state, trying to relieve her nerves.

"Hi, I can't believe I look very beautiful right now," she says with a giggle, trying to bury her face in my bicep.

"You always look beautiful," I announce truthfully.

She lifts her head and looks at me seriously. "Thank you." Leaning to me she places her lips against mine in a gentle kiss. I deepen the kiss before she can pull away, worrying about morning breath.

Ed's fist banging on the door as he passes causes us to break apart. "Wake up sleepyhead. We're going for a run, remember?" he asks as I hear him close the bathroom door.

"Do you have to go?" Ruby complains. "I'm sure we can come up with another form of exercise without even having to leave the bed."

"As tempting as that is, Ed will kill me if I stand him up," I say kissing her on the head as I pull my arm from under her. I hear Ed leave the bathroom, so I quickly grab some clothes so I can jump in the shower and wash away the smell of all we'd been up to last night. I don't want Ed and other weres picking up on what we've been doing.

By the time I make it back into the bedroom Ruby is dressed in the sexy brown dress she'd been wearing yesterday, the one that got her into my bed in the first place. She pulls the covers tidy over the bed, leaning over to brush one stubborn corner over. Sneaking up behind her I grab the thigh that she's unintentionally flashing, making her jump.

"You know, I really like this dress," I say, my hand working its way little higher.

"Ah huh, you have a run to go on, remember? You lost all rights to touching when you turned down my offer of a day in bed," she says giggling as she ducks under my arm and makes a run for it through the door.

I follow her through the tiny house heading for the kitchen taking slow and deliberate steps, trying to keep my wolf calm because he likes the chase. I don't want him to start thinking of her as prey. I've already had a close call with Rosabel a couple of months ago, I don't need the embarrassment of doing the same thing with Ruby. I'll never live it down. As soon as she reaches the doorway, I grab her around the waist and pull her back against my front. She squeals as I nuzzle at her neck.

"I've got you, now what shall I do with you?"

"I've told you, you gave up the chance of having me in bed all day. So get all those dirty ideas out of your head," Ruby says as I reluctantly let her go, remembering too late we aren't the only ones in the room. I look up and catch Ed's nostrils flare before he storms out of the house without saying a word to either of us. He'd be able to smell last night on Ruby. I shouldn't be surprised by his reaction, I know he wants Ruby for himself. He hasn't said so, but I can see it in the way he watches her. It's the same way I watch her.

"Why does he hate me so much?" Ruby complains watching the closed door Eddie just stormed out of. "It's as if he can't even stand to be in the same room as me anymore. He was the first pack member that saw me as me, and not just Theo's kid sister."

I wish she didn't care what he thought about her, but it's something that's never going to change, they both care about each other too much and they can't even see it. I'm now kicking myself for taking it that step further last night. I'd be lying if I said that wanting to make sure I was ready for a mate was the only thing holding me back. The thought of Ed and his feelings for her are evident to me, no matter how well he tries to hide it. Plus, it was pretty common knowledge that Ruby had a crush on him a while back, they played a big part in my waiting. I should never have slept with her. I was kidding myself thinking it would work between Ruby and me.

"He doesn't hate you, that's the problem," I say pacing across the small kitchen. My wolf is pulsing at my skin as he picks up on my agitation.

This isn't going to work; I'm not the one she loves.

If I don't stop this now we're all going to walk away with broken hearts, and that's with the hope I'm not already too late.

"I can't do this anymore, last night was a mistake," I blurt out, not giving myself time to back out of my decision.

"What…what are you talking about?" Ruby asks, clearly confused by my outburst.

I say the only thing that I know will send her running. "We can't stay together anymore. I need to wait for my true mate. I need what Theo has."

Ruby is barely out the door when I pull my phone out and hit call to the one person I know can comfort her.

16. PUSHING THE WOLF DOWN
Eddie

I wish I could be happy for them, but I just can't. My wolf believes Ruby should be our mate and he'd happily tear Paddy to shreds to make that point perfectly clear and I'm not allowing him to kill my best mate.

No fucking chance.

If that means I have to leave the room or even the house, every time they enter all lovey dovey smelling of sex, then that's how it's going to be. I don't care how fucked up it is. It's better than the other option.

The vibration of my phone pulls my thoughts away from the argument I'm having with my wolf, and causes me to slow my pace to pull out my phone. Seeing Paddy's name on the screen I consider not answering for a second, but duty to the pack and my best mate forces me to answer. "This better be good, I already need a fucking drink and it's not even nine in the morning."

"You need to go find Ruby. She ran off and I can't go after her."

"Fix your own damn problems, Paddy. Whatever you've done she'll get over it soon enough. Just go after her," I offer, knowing she won't be mad at him for long, no matter what he's done. She was head over heels with him this morning.

"No, you don't understand. We're over. I was fooling myself from the start, she was always yours."

Hearing everything I need, I hang up and run back to the duplex hoping to catch her scent. It only takes me a couple of seconds to catch it and follow. It's leading out of town and into the surrounding bush. Walking through some trees I spot her, looking beautiful in the middle of the field with the mountains in front of her and her golden ringlets blowing in the wind.

Once I reach her, I can hear her sobs. Turning Ruby around, I pull her into my chest. "Let it out, Rubes."

Time passes quietly as she lets all her tears out, with just the rustle of the wind in the trees and the grass, and the odd cockatoo calling its mate to be heard. "How could he do that? Why make love to me if he knew he wanted to find his true mate? Because no matter what he says now, he made love to me last night…" she pauses just long enough to take a breath before carrying on, "I thought he was going to take me as a mate, we'd talked about it." A new wave of fresh tears start as she sobs into my chest once again. My heart tears in two at the thought of them making love. I should be the only one making love to her.

"I don't know why he'd do that, sweetheart, he's a stupid dick." My comment turns her sob into a giggle.

"Where have you been?" she asks looking up at me with her big green eyes.

"I've been right here, waiting for you to need me," I say as I kiss her on the forehead, feeling stripped bare by the look in her eyes.

"I've always needed you, Eddie."

My breath catches with her words, and my wolf tries to take her as ours. Forcing him down, I squeeze her in our hug a little tighter not knowing how else to react without being inappropriate. She's not going to want more than a friend right now. I just wish my wolf would understand that.

We stand a while longer as she calms down, the tears ease slowing their tracks down her cheeks. She pulls out of my hold and stands back from me, before silently walking over to a fallen tree and perching her arse on it. I follow her lead and do the same. Seeing I'm settled she turns her head to look at me, her whole demeanour changing.

I feel the anger coming off her before she opens her mouth. "What did I do to make you treat me like shit over the last few weeks?"

Her question causes my mind to run around in circles. *Do I tell her the truth?* No, I can't tell her the truth, not without coming across as a fucking creeper hitting on her when she's just been dumped. The truth is out of the question, but that doesn't help me work out what to actually tell her. I lift my head and look at the tree line opposite us hoping for some inspiration.

It's so peaceful here, how have I never noticed that before?

Making my mind up on what to say, I plaster on my most flirtatious smile, before opening my mouth, "You know me, Rubes, I don't know how to interact with a chick without flirting. I didn't want Paddy challenging me for it, I thought you'd miss him if I killed him." I throw her a wink and get a thump in the arm for my trouble.

"You're terrible, Eddie," she says, seemingly taking me at my word. The glint in her eye is telling me she's not entirely convinced, but her anger has dissipated so I'll take that as a win.

She leans her head against my shoulder and stares of at the tree line I'd just been looking at. "I've missed you and your cheeky ways."

She'll never have a chance to miss my cheeky ways again because I'm not going anywhere. The last few weeks have been hell for me, and I can't do that again.

17. UNEXPECTED HEART TO HEART
Ruby

After Eddie let me cry on his shoulder for most of the day, he walked me back to Theo's. I had no idea there were tracks through the bush from their place to Theo's. Although after he had explained about the many tracks leading from Theo's place to almost everywhere in town for the pack to use in emergencies, it made complete sense. I spent the rest of the day in bed, crying and wondering where I'd gone wrong in reading Paddy and his feelings while dozing on and off.

I wake up to a dark room, reaching out I feel about on the bedside table blindly until I grip my phone, lifting it up glimpsing at the time. One in the morning, and I'm wide awake. *Brilliant.*

Knowing I won't fall straight back to sleep, I decide to go downstairs and make myself a chamomile tea. Walking through the house in the dark, I try to do everything as quietly as possible. Living in a house full of people is bad enough when three of those people are weres it's even worse. I hear footsteps padding on the carpet of the hall and curse myself for not just staying in bed. I'm really not in the mood for company right now. I don't even know if anyone but Eddie knows about what happened between me and Paddy.

I turn to see Selena enter the kitchen, giving me a small smile. "I'm sorry if I woke you up, I was trying to be quiet," I apologise as I pour the boiled water over the tea bag in my cup.

"You didn't wake me up, this little mister likes to keep me awake, it's become our nightly ritual," she says patting her swollen stomach lovingly as she shuffles toward the cupboard and reaches down a cup.

"Do you want chamomile?" I ask holding up a tea bag. She nods. "Please."

I pour her tea and remove the tea bag from my cup, throwing the used tea bag in the rubbish bin under the counter, before giving the one in Selena's cup the same treatment. We silently walk over to the L-shaped sofa's and take a seat beside each other, both shuffling about to find comfortable positions. I sit back in the corner with my feet folded under me as Selena sits at the end turning herself slightly to face me while propping her feet on the coffee table.

"We've determined the cause of my lack of sleep. What's keeping you up?" she asks as she takes a sip from the cup she's nursing between her hands.

"It's a long story," I brush her off, not knowing where to start or whether I even want to go into it. Especially with Selena, she doesn't even know about the wolves, so how would I start talking about mates and such things.

"Neither of us have anything better to do. I'm more than happy to listen, it'll make a nice change to the lonely nights I normally have," she offers.

Seeing the genuine look on her face I make a decision, I hope, I won't regret later.

"I broke up with my boyfriend this morning. Right after we slept together for the first time." Even I cringe at the bitterness in my voice.

"I'm sorry to hear that, Ruby. Any breakup is hard, but it's even harder after a night of loving."

I glance at her sharply. *How does she know it was lovingly?*

As if reading my mind, she answers the question that must be plastered on my face. "I've seen you and Paddy together over the last few weeks. I saw the way he looks at you. There's no way he wouldn't show you that love the first time you slept together."

"Yeah, well, he said he was waiting for his..." I manage to stop myself saying, true mate. "Waiting for the one," I correct myself.

"Finding the one is overrated. I learnt that the hard way. I had a good thing with Theo, it wasn't perfect, there were a lot of secrets between us, there still are, but you can live with secrets if they don't hurt you. I went and ruined all that finding my one. When he realised what we had, he couldn't destroy his brother's life, even though he knew we were meant to be."

Is she talking about Cain? She cheated on Theo with our brother Cain, he left straight after it happened. No one knows where he is, Theo has a number to contact him but I don't know if he'll ever use it. If what she's saying is true, and Cain left so he wouldn't destroy Theo's life, he was too late, sleeping with his wife already achieved that.

"Enough about me," she says with a shake of her head. "What are you going to do to get him back?"

"That didn't work well for you," I say before really thinking about my words. She takes in a sharp breath as though my words wounded her somehow. "I'm sorry, you didn't deserve that."

"No, you're right. It didn't matter how much love Theo and I had for each other, it wasn't enough. I couldn't get him to forgive me. I came back with the one thing he always wanted from me, hoping it would be sufficient for his forgiveness but I was too late, he'd met his true love." The sadness in her eyes gives me a whole new respect for her.

How can she live under the same roof as her ex-husband and his fiancée?

"How do you do it? How do you live with them?"

Taking a moment to have a sip from her cup, no doubt giving herself time to think of how to answer such a loaded question, she slowly looks across at me ensuring eye contact while she answers. It's almost like she's laying herself out there for me to see everything she feels. "I'm not going to lie and say it doesn't hurt. But in saying that, anyone can see they're meant to be, that's why I gave him the divorce without a fight. I couldn't stand in the way of love like that. And if I'm being honest, my heart belongs to someone else. It always has." She reaches up and absently wipes a tear from her cheek. "We've ended up on me again," she laughs quietly. "With Paddy's connection to Theo, he'll be around a lot. Can you handle that?" The way she said the word *connection* made me watch her with suspicion. She has never been told about the wolves, she always believed anyone he had over was a work colleague or friend. That every full moon when Theo was away for the night and sometimes the following day, he was on a business trip. We've always joked that she must be so dumb to fall for something like that, but looking at her now I'm starting to wonder if she's smarter than we've given her credit for. "He works at the gym doesn't he? Theo always treated his employees like family." With those words I realise my mind is playing tricks on me. I was giving her way too much credit.

"I thought I heard voices," Mum says from behind us startling us both, so much so I slosh my now lukewarm tea all down front.

"Shit!" I curse.

"Was it hot?" she asks as she runs into the kitchen and grabs a tea-towel.

"No, it's fine, just wet. We didn't mean to wake anyone," I reassure her as I dab at the wet patch with the tea-towel she hands over.

"The chamomile seems to have put the little mister to sleep, so I'm going to try and get a couple of hours sleep," Selena says as she gets up with a groan. "This chair is too soft, if I get any bigger I'll never get up. Night ladies."

Mum takes the seat Selena left and reaching out she gives my hand a squeeze before dropping it again. "I'm sorry to hear about Paddy."

"How long were you listening?" I ask shocked at the thought of her listening in to our conversation. I had thought the others in the house might overhear the conversation with their were-animal hearing, but I'd never considered my mum listening in.

"I'm sorry. I heard talking and when I came down you were both saying personal things and it didn't seem right to interrupt. It sounded like Selena needed to get some things off her chest as much as you did."

"What do you want, Mum?" I insist. Knowing there has to be a reason she's sitting here now, she could have just gone to back to bed and I'd be non-the-wiser about her eavesdropping.

"My therapist insists I be honest. Especially with you, since it's you I've harmed the most. I put you in so much danger over the years bringing back all those strangers. I don't blame you for hating me."

"The strangers that snuck into my room after you'd passed out. Those same strangers that I had to fight off night after night." I angrily wipe away the tear that runs down my cheek. "The one that caught me when I was weak with a fever, the one who stole away my virginity. Yeah, Mum, that's right, he stole the one thing I was meant to save for the one I love." The tears are now streaming down my face, I don't bother trying to wipe at them. "Not that that really matters anymore, because the guy I loved enough to share myself with just dumped me after I had sex with him, so if I'd saved it for him it would've been wasted anyway." I stop talking to quickly catch my breath. "Who knows maybe you did me a favour after all."

She pulls me into her arms and I go, too broken to put up a fight.

The tears eventually ease and I pull away to sit back, only to realise I wasn't the only one crying all that time. "It looks like we both let out enough tears to fill a bathtub," I say with a giggle.

"I know you had to guard your words with Selena. I just want you to know you have someone to talk to, who isn't going to instantly be on his side because they share the werewolf gene. I'm human just like you, and I understand them and the issues they can bring to a relationship."

"Thanks Mum. I don't even know what to say about it anymore. I know I'm not his true mate, so I have to respect his decision. It just stings. Mainly because we spoke about it, he said he didn't care about waiting for his true mate. Some wolves wait all their lives for their true mate and never find them. We held off being intimate for that reason, he wanted to make sure he was committed to me. Then we go there and he changes his mind." I feel like I'm talking myself in circles, my mind is running ninety miles an hour.

"I think it's for the best. There's nothing worse than him finding his true mate after he's mated with you. That's what happened between your father and me."

Stunned at her admission, I can't help but jump in. "I thought he was all for the pack?"

"Of all the werewolves you know, tell me, would any of them leave their mate in one town bringing up his kids, while he lived in another town surrounded by his pack. Remember, he was an alpha too. Would Theo do that?"

Thinking about what she was saying for a minute, I realise I've never really considered how he lived that far away from his mate. Of all the mated couples I know, not one of them would live like that. "He had his true mate with him in the pack," I say stating the obvious.

Mum nods with a sad smile. "Her name was Margaret."

"You knew about her? True mates are notorious for killing the other mate, how did you survive?" The questions fall out of my mouth one after another.

"I only had Theodore when she arrived on the scene. She wasn't willing to bring him up as her own and your father wouldn't let her kill him. She couldn't hold a child to term so after a number of miscarriages he came back to me for more children. I don't know how he talked her into that, but somehow he did. I'm just grateful it didn't come down to a death match because I would've had no chance."

Seeing the light coming in through the windows, I realise it must be getting close to everyone's alarms going off. "I guess we should both try and squeeze in an hour's worth of sleep or we won't be up to much company today."

Mum glances down at her watch before slowly standing alongside me. "It's good that it's coming close to the end of spring and the sun is coming up earlier than normal. We might get a couple of hours sleep before we have to be up."

Before heading up the stairs, I give her a quick hug. "Thanks for the chat," I whisper in her ear. She squeezes me back tightly, before heading off to the front of the house where she's sleeping in one of the bedrooms, neighbouring both Selena and Jared.

18. SHOPPING MAKES HUNGRY MEN
Ruby

"Who's babysitting today, boys?" I enquire, walking into the lounge. After my heart to heart with my mum and Selena yesterday, I feel much better. I can't help noticing that Paddy is missing. *Does that mean he's miserable?* It may make me a bitch, but I hope he's hurting, even if it's just a little.

Ed shuffles over giving me room to sit next to him. "That all depends on what you have planned. I'm not doing a spa day ever again. I still have that stinky shit causing my nose problems," he says referring to our previous spa visit.

I open my mouth before my brain kicks in, "But I bet the ladies like the smooth chest."

The stunned look on his face makes me realise what I've just said. I slip my hand up to cover my mouth too late.

The guys burst into laughter. "You…had a wax?" Jared asks between his laughter.

"For fuck's sake, Ruby, that was supposed to be between us," Ed complains. He looks around at the boys; Jared, Wes, and Matthew. "They made me do it, they wouldn't let me stand guard if not. I took one for the team." They were all too busy laughing to even listen to his reasoning. *Poor Eddie.*

"You want to think yourselves lucky it wasn't you. I know each and every one of you would've done the same if you were in his shoes," Bel says effectively silencing the guys as she enters the room. "You're all off the hook because we're dress shopping today. I've been told I can't get married in jeans and a T-shirt," she adds with a roll of her eyes.

The guys all get up whooping at the thought of a free day. "Let's go shoot some pool," Matthew suggests. With nods of agreement, they all start to leave.

"Jared, can I have a quick word?" Bel asks.

I catch her eye and nod toward the other room, offering to leave them to have a private conversation, or as private a conversation one can get in a house full of werewolves. "Stay where you are, Rubes, it's nothing private."

Jared turns in the doorway and glances at the chair he'd just occupied. "Should I be sitting for this?" he asks sounding nervous. "You're going to tell me to go home aren't you? My dad calls every day telling me the same thing, so don't waste your breath." I've never heard him sound so defeated. *What the hell is going on with him?*

Bel pulls him into a hug. "I don't want you to go. If I were selfish, I would demand you never leave. But I can't do that, the pride will need you one day but today isn't it."

"Really?" he asks leaning back to look her in the eyes, no doubt seeking the truth. Whatever he sees must be enough because with a short, sharp nod he releases her and steps back. "So, what did you want to talk to me about?"

"I don't know how to ask," Bel admits as she fiddles with a strand of cotton hanging from the hem of her T-shirt.

"Just spit it out," he says playfully as he reaches forward to tuck a stray piece of hair behind her ear. "Sorry, old habits," he apologises realising what he's done.

"Be my man of honour," she blurts out.

He takes a step back, surprise written all over his face. "What?"

Bel turns away and paces across the room, before turning back to face Jared. "If you were a girl, you'd be my maid of honour. So be my man of honour, please?" she begs.

"Okay," he replies with a nod before Bel throws herself at him.

"Thank you."

"I'm not wearing a dress," he scoffs, grinning at me over her shoulder. "I draw the line at that!"

***

We spent all day traipsing around the bridal shops of Sydney. Rosabel has tried so many dresses on that I've lost count, and here we are back in the first shop we started in.

I never want to get married!

"Baby Bel, I love you. But I swear, if I have to go to one more shop I won't be held accountable for my actions," Jared complains once again. He'd said the same thing three shops ago.

Bel is standing in the middle of the room on the platform as she looks at herself in the mirrors wearing the beautiful lace covered dress. "This is the one."

Jared walks around her giving her a thorough once over. "You look stunning, Bel. Theo isn't going to know what hit him," he says, his voice full of pride.

I glance at Misty, who like me, has her eyes brimming with tears. I can only manage a nod in agreement, I don't think I can get any words out through the lump in my throat.

Misty and I chose dresses at this shop the first time around. They are a lovely purple colour with a sweetheart cut. So, thankfully, we don't have any more to worry about since the shopkeeper has all the payment and fitting details.

Leaving Bel to undress, we head to the main sales room. "Who's opening the bar tonight Misty?" I question, glancing the time on the clock. There's no chance we'll make it back in time.

"Lucy's opening up and Theo said he'd get a couple of the lads to help her out until we get back," she answers. "It's mid-week so I'm sure they'll manage just fine."

"Eddie messaged me earlier asking how long we'd be. So I'm pretty sure he's one of the guys Theo is sending." His phone makes a noise and he pulls it out and laughs as he reads the screen. "Looks like Paddy drew the other short straw. Good, they need some time to sort their shit out. Let's grab dinner on the way home. All this shopping has made me hungry."

His comment about Paddy and Eddie catches my attention. "They're best mates, what shit have they got to sort out?" I haven't seen them having issues. Eddie was off with me for a while, but he explained all that when he let me fall apart on him the other day. I hope he isn't being pissy at Paddy for treating me like that. I don't want to be the cause of their problems.

Bel chooses that moment to come out of the fitting room and throw an arm over my shoulders. "Boy stuff. Where do you want to eat, Rubes?" She dismisses my question. *Fine,* I'll drop the issue for now, but if I sense any tension between them, I'll be putting an end to it.

"The Irish pub across the road looks like it could be good," I say with a shrug as we exit the building. I'd been watching people leaving through the window, for the last few minutes while Bel got changed, they all looked pretty happy. So the place can't be that bad. With nods of agreement we all make our way across the road.

Jared holds open the door as we each enter. "You girls grab a table and some menus, and I'll get the drinks."

We choose a quiet booth at the back of the dining area, Bel and Misty slide into one side and I glide into the other. I glance across at the girls and it suddenly dawns on me, I've never had a drink with Misty and Bel before.

Jared places four glasses down and sits down next to me. "What does the menu look like?" he asks.

"So good, I can't decide what to have," Bel declares not taking her eyes off the menu in her hands. "It was a good idea grabbing dinner on the way home."

Misty places hers on the table, sliding it across to Jared. "Have a look, I know what I'm having."

Taking the menu, Jared places it on the table between us so we can both see it clearly. Spotting the fish and chips, my decision is made and I push the menu so it's in front of Jared.

"I'm good."

While Jared and Bel make their decisions, I look over to Misty and ask her something I've often wondered. "How come you don't do food at Misty's? You'd make a killing with all the hungry werewolves you have in there."

"I can't cook," she says like it's an obvious reason.

"What about hiring someone?"

She looks at me flabbergasted. "Do ya know how hard it is to find someone who knows about the supernatural creatures and can cook a decent meal? It's nigh-on impossible."

"I could do it. I'd need a bracelet to get in, but you made one for Benji easy enough," I offer on instinct. I've always liked to cook, I've never thought about making a career out of it though, but it's got to be better than cleaning up after my brother. Watching Misty think it over and feeling the butterflies in my stomach makes me realise how much I really want this chance.

Bel looks at me, concern written in the furrow of her brow and he pursing of her lips. "What about your criminology course?" Geez, it's like she's channelling Theo if he were here that's exactly what he would say.

"It's an online course I can do it anytime, I'm not working." I can't hold back my defensive tone. "I know you're only saying what Theo would, but he has to accept that I'm not a little kid anymore. I'm a grown arse woman and I'm allowed to make my own decisions."

Bel glances down at the table, seemingly hurt. "I wasn't implying anything by what I said. I just wanted to make sure you'd thought about it."

I pat her hand over the table. "I'm sorry, Bel, I shouldn't have taken my anger at Theo out on you."

She smiles grateful for my apology.

"Well, I think it's a great idea. Shall we give it a trial run, starting tomorrow?" Misty offers. "I'll make ya a bracelet when I get home tonight, I can't believe I haven't given ya one yet."

I can't hide the excitement from my voice. "I'd love that."

Bel bangs her hand on the table, making me jump. "Hey, we have a movie date tomorrow," she complains.

Misty waves her hand in at the table. "What did that table do to ya?" She laughs, before making an offer. "Go tonight, I'll get one of the guys to stick around when I get back if need be."

Bel and I look at each other and nod our agreement.

"Thanks, Misty," Bel says, gratefully.

A pretty blonde waitress steps up to our table with a pen and pad. "Are you ready to order?" she asks, blatantly eyeing up Jared. You can't take these guys anywhere without them catching someone's eye.

Jared throws her a wink. "We certainly are, sweetheart."

I listen to them flirt with each other and can't help but smile. I suddenly realise I really I'm okay without Paddy, maybe we weren't meant to be after all. Blondie takes our orders without taking her eyes off Jared. It's going to be interesting to see what meals we actually receive.

19. BLACKNESS DESCENDS
Ruby

We walk out the movies giggling at how I managed to trip up the stairs and face plant on the floor while dashing back from a bathroom break. I can never get through a movie without having to dash to the bathroom. I blame the Coke.

"Ruby. One second…you were there, the next…you were gone," Bel manages to spit out between fits of laughter. "I thought you'd turned vamp or gained a druid's power of teleporting in and out whenever and wherever they want. Until I heard the grunt as you got up." The laughter starts again.

"I wish that was the case," I say, hating the embarrassed feeling I have. I can't help but wish I was a werewolf like Bel. She's so graceful and has such good instincts she would never have fallen so stupidly. It isn't the first time I've found myself wishing I was a werewolf. Having two werewolf brothers, I've often wished I wasn't the human of the three of us. The ugly duckling.

"I better get home before Theo sends someone after me," I say. "He's more like a prison guard than a brother," I add.

"He just worries about you. You're a fragile human, give him a little slack, hey? Tell him, I'll be home soon. I love the fact that I've moved in with him, but I hate this packing business, and I didn't come to town with a lot of stuff," Bel says, hugging me goodbye. I watch as she dematerialises before my eyes. That druid blood she recently discovered has come in pretty handy at times.

Having parked my car at the other end of the main road means I have a good ten-minute walk ahead of me. Normally that would be okay, but we've just watched a horror movie about vampires. You'd think knowing vampires are real would make movies about them laughable, but it's because I know the monsters are real that it scares me.

I start walking at a fast pace, hearing nothing but the click-clack of my heels on the pavement.

Click-clack...

Click-clack...

Click-clack...

The hairs on the back of my neck stand on end and a shiver runs down my back.

I freeze on the spot and look around having no idea what I expect to see. I don't have the sense of smell a werewolf has or the hearing of a vampire, but I do have the gut instinct of a human and mine is speaking to me right now - telling me to get the hell out of there. I do just that.

I run across the road not even looking for passing traffic. Luckily it's clear.

Once my feet touch the pavement, I notice all the feeling of worry has gone. I look around again and could slap myself upside the head. I'd been so distracted that I hadn't noticed during our giggles we'd crossed the road and ended up outside Misty's, a bar that caters only for supes. It's owned by a witch who puts wards on it that scare the bejesus out of humans, so they don't, won't, and can't enter. It's impossible. What if a supe carried them over the threshold kicking and screaming? I hear you ask. A human's heart would just stop beating. Dead. Misty has been known to make some specially warded bracelets that allow a human to enter, but only for a few special people. I'm going to be one of those people tomorrow, and I'll be starting my new job as a chef. I can't wait to get home and tell Theo my news.

I start walking again laughing at my stupidity, letting a silly horror movie distract me enough to not notice Misty's. I know my car isn't that far up the road. Another five minutes at the most. I start listening to the click clack of my heels again.

Click-clack....

Click-clack....

Click click clack clack.

I hear double footsteps in quick succession. Knowing I'm not walking fast enough to warrant that means only one thing - someone is following me.

"You might as well come out. I know you're there," I speak into the darkness, not bothering to raise my voice knowing whichever wolf my brother has sent would have no trouble hearing me even if I whispered. But I get no response.

I stop and turn to face behind me, where they must be hiding in a shadow or the eave of a building because I can't see anyone, but I speak up anyway.

"I won't tell Theo that you weren't covert enough."

Werewolves can move without being heard. This one was obviously being sloppy for a human to have heard them following me.

I still get no response, so I give up and turn around starting for my car. I can see it across the road when I'm suddenly grabbed from behind. An arm around my waist, the other hand over my mouth mutes my screams. The person holding me drags me into a dark alley between the shops. I'm pinned against the wall face first. All I can see is the bare red bricks of the wall.

The hand over my mouth pulls my head to the side stretching my neck out, as the arm around my waist disappears.

I wriggle to get free, but I'm still pinned in place by the body behind me, as hard and strong as the wall in front. I feel the hand that had been around my waist, brush my long blonde curls from my neck. He strokes over my pulse with his fingers.

It's then that I realise I'm not just trapped by a psycho, I'm trapped by a vampire.

That recognition hits a second before the fingers disappear and sharp fangs pierce my neck. The pain is horrendous. I can feel my heart beat rise with fear.

I bite down hard on the hand over my mouth trying to distract the vampire at my neck. I attempt to fight with my body, but I don't have the room to move. The only thing I'm succeeding in is raising my pulse therefore giving the vampire a faster and easier meal.

My mind starts to become sluggish, listening to the vampire moan as he sucks my veins dry makes me push the fog back and try to think of a way out of this. If I don't do something quick, I won't survive this.

If I were a werewolf, I'd have the strength to get away, is the last coherent thought that runs through my mind before blackness descends.

20. GIFT FROM HELL
Dominick

I forgo my standard mode of transportation, teleportation and decide a brisk walk home from Misty's would do me good. I've needed to clear my head for a while. As much as I love my people, they don't give me much space to do such a thing. Being in no hurry to get home, a walk seems like a good idea.

Home. Home is a large compound where me and my vampires all live together. A few handpicked humans live on the premises as well. They offer us blood in return for a home and protection. I often wonder if I should follow some of the other kings and live a more solitary life. I never wonder for long, I know solitary living isn't for me. I tried that a long time ago and it's a sure path to insanity. As much as I like some time to myself, I need to be surrounded by people. By family.

The smell of fresh blood pulls me out of my musings. As I take in my surroundings, I'm surprised to be in the alley leading to the compound. Taking uncertain steps into the shadows, I spot a body laid haphazardly across the doorstep.

The scent of werewolf hits me at full force and I can't help but panic. If this is one of Theo's werewolves, shit is going to hit the fan. The blonde is face down, so I reach out my hand and pull her over, I need to see her face and when I do I wish I could erase the sight of it. He's changed his MO. Her forehead has the word *'with'* etched into it, and her right cheek has the word *'love.'* It's the *'JD x'* etched into her left cheek that throws me for a loop. All this time I've thought he's just some random vampire bored with the rules. Never did I think it was JD, Jay Dawes. The same JD that was once my human lover. Once I look past the initials and see the face, a face I recognise as Theodore Wilson's sister, Ruby, I shake my head. *Focus dammit.* She may still be alive. I don't bother trying to listen for her heartbeat, I probably wouldn't hear it over my own anyway. Instead, I pick up her wrist and pierce her flesh with my fangs, tasting her blood, hoping to feel the warm liquid flow down my throat. It isn't flowing, but her life force is there, her soul is hanging on. She's so close to death, there's no saving her from it completely, but I can save her from permanent death. I can sire her.

Make her one of us, one of *mine*.

I haven't sired anyone for centuries. I vouched that I would never sire anyone again. Not after I lost my one love. The thought of leaving her to die, lingers in my mind for a minute, before I tear at my own wrist and place it to her lips. My blood and life force flowing into her mouth.

I bang on the door beside me with my free fist, *"Niko!"* I shout.

The door opens and Niko is immediately by my side. "We need to get her inside and lying down."

He picks her up and cradles her in his arm as I tear at my wrist once again and place it back over her mouth before we awkwardly move into the lounge room closest to the entrance.

Ruby clamps her mouth on my wrist as Niko lays her on one of the sofas. That's a good sign, she's accepting the change. Her body is anyway. Deep down her soul or spirit is too, but when she wakes up, she'll have no idea what's happened.

Over 2000 years ago.

I opened my eyes to such brightness, I could only hiss in pain as I closed them tightly.

"Put out the fire, you idiot!" a female screamed.

I clamped a hand over my ears, it felt like she'd yelled directly into my eardrums, but I could feel that there was no one close enough to do that. I knew where people were in the room, it felt like nothing I'd ever experienced before, almost like ants crawling on my skin. I didn't understand how it told me where exactly they were positioned, but I just knew it did.

"Dominick? Feed!" The voice demanded and I couldn't do anything but follow the command. My mouth opened and I felt pain along my jaw but didn't have time to think about it, because soon the most divine tasting liquid was flowing over my tongue and down my gullet.

Whatever had been clamped in my mouth was suddenly torn away, for a moment I wanted to fight for it. I needed it back. But that voice poured over me once again commanding me to be calm. "That's enough for now, you'll get some more soon. I promise."

I opened my eyes once again and saw the beautiful monster before me. Taking stock of my body and my senses, I knew I wasn't the person I had once been. Somehow I'd been changed, changed into whatever this creature before me was.

***

I tear open my wrist for what feels like the millionth time, but before I can place it back over Ruby's mouth Niko grabs it and glares at me. "That's enough! If you give her any more of your blood, you won't see tomorrow."

Pulling my hand from his makes the world spin. I realise that he's right. I've almost drained myself dry. *Shit.*

I'd lost myself in my memories. I've lived for so long, I never allow myself to think of the past, there's too much pain to wallow there.

"Feed," a female voice commands as a wrist presses against my lips. My fangs elongate but it's so close to my memories, I can't blindly sink my fangs in. Even though I know the voice is Sam, I need to see it's her. I look across the room to where the voice is coming from and see Sam before I turn my eyes to the person who the hand belongs to. Gerry. I flash back to a couple of nights ago when we shared a night of passion. My fangs ache, at the memory of his blood flowing over my tongue. If I don't feed soon, bloodlust may take over and that wouldn't be good.

His small smile of encouragement makes me pause, he's my lover, he deserves more intimacy than for me to draw from his wrist. I don't have the energy to take this somewhere else, but I change my position so I'm sitting on the floor with my back against the couch. I beckon for him to lay against my front between my legs, giving me access to his neck. The smile he gives me in return confirms I'm doing the right thing.

As he gets himself comfy and tilts his head giving me access to the vein in his neck, I command the others to leave the room. "Niko, ensure everyone knows not to enter for the rest of the night."

Everyone but Niko leaves the room without argument.

"Of course. What about the girl?" he asks, nodding his head toward her lifeless body.

"I've done all I can for her, we won't know if it's worked until she comes around tomorrow night. If she comes around." I don't want to think about her not coming around. Or the conversation I need to have with the alpha mutt. I might not like the guy, but I wouldn't wish this on him.

"Would you like me to move her?" he asks.

"If you could see to organising a room for her, I'll bring her when I'm done here," I say dismissing him as I lean my head forward and lick at Gerry's neck, to make sure he's ready for my fangs, before sinking them in and taking my fill, while allowing my hands to roam over his body and feeling how much he's enjoying this.

21. CALLING THE ENEMY
Dominick

I settle Ruby down in the bed that will be hers for as long as she needs or wants it. If she wakes. No, I'm not allowing that to be a possibility. *When* she wakes, she'll be a vampire and *my* vampires will always have a home at the compound.

I take a seat at the desk in the corner of the room and pull my phone out. Calling that furry mutt is the last thing I want to do. But he'll start worrying soon and I only have a short window to tell him what's happened before I'm out of action for the day. I find his name in my contacts list, press call and put the phone to my ear.

He answers immediately. "I don't have time for any shit, Drake. What do you want?"

"Let me guess, that beautiful little sister of yours hasn't made curfew? Do they still call it curfew these—"

"How the fuck do you know that?" he demands cutting me off mid-sentence. "If you've done something to her, not even Bel can hold me back from killing you for it." He has every right to dish out the threats.

"You might want to listen to what I have to say before you start with the threats," he growls down the phone.

"I'm listening."

I take a breath I don't need and let it all out. "I came home to find another gift waiting on my doorstep. It...it was Ruby."

"*No!* You're wrong," he denies immediately, as though he won't even allow the idea in his mind.

"Theo, I'm sorry. I'm not mistaken. It's Ruby." I can't hide the sympathy in my voice.

"Is she?" Knowing all the others had been dead when they were found, I can understand him jumping to that conclusion.

I kick myself for not making him aware of her status sooner. "She was so close to death, Theo. Too close. I couldn't stop it...I...The only way I could save her was to turn her. She's currently going through the transition."

The silence on the end of the phone is unnerving. I'd thought he would've had some form of an outburst after I'd finished.

"Did you hear what I said?" I ask the sound of his breathing is the only sign he's still on the other end of the phone.

"I heard you. She's dead," he says, his voice void of any emotion. He sounds...deadly. I've never been scared of the wolf but hearing him like that has me on edge.

"If it works she'll be a vampire. She'll still be here on this earth. Hell, she can still live with you if she wants. Nothing has to change," I say, trying to get something out of him. I know he hates us, but surely he'd rather his sister be here, even as a vampire, than completely cease to exist?

"Everything has changed. She can never come here, it's a sanctuary for pack members. I can't let a vampire in here. Our scent will drive her crazy, I can't allow her to feed on pack members, just like I don't allow any of you bloodsuckers too. I don't care if she *was* once my baby sister," he says flatly.

Fuck!

That's not going to help her transition, if she wakes up and has her brother and the pack waiting for her, she could fight the bloodlust. But if she wakes up and finds out she's been as good as disowned, she has nothing to fight for. I say as much to the furry mutt.

"Your sister is strong, she'll fight the bloodlust. She'll do it for you. For the pack."

"She isn't pack anymore. She's yours," he says. "She isn't mine," I hear him whisper before disconnecting the call, those three words were full of the emotion his earlier words had been missing.

He's right in the fact that she's one of mine. I'll make sure she has something to fight for. She'll prove how strong she can be to that furry mutt.

I watch the female for a moment hoping that the unseen magic is doing all it can to change her body so it will stay forever young and beautiful. Knowing Ruby won't wake up until well into the night, I don't worry about leaving her alone throughout the day. I head to my room and allow myself the recuperation that vampires receive from dying for the day. Essentially that's what we do, we die with the sunrise and reanimate with the sunset, the older you are, the longer you can last between those hours. I open my door to find a small body curled in the sheets waiting for me, exactly where I'd left him after I'd had my fill earlier.

22. THE WORLD SHATTERS
Eddie

I'm standing in Theo's dining room-come-pack meeting room, with Billy, Jared, And Wes. They all look just as clueless as I feel, our eyes are darting between each other. I'd received a phone call from Theo, ten minutes ago, he muttered the word *'emergency'* before hanging up. Hearing the front door open we all turn and watch Paddy enter.

"What's happening?" Paddy asks.

"Your guess is as good as ours," Wes mutters flatly.

We all feel Theo's energy as he approaches the room. By the time he's in sight, we know this is serious.

The hackles rise on my wolf.

Our alpha isn't in a good place he's on the edge of losing control, which in turn, makes our wolves testy.

Bel comes in chasing after him. "Theo! Take a second to calm down." She overtakes and stops in front of him, causing him to halt mid-stride. "Babe, please," she pleads with a comforting hand pressed against his chest. "Once you tell them, they're all going to be struggling with control enough as it is. They don't need your wolf's anger pushed on them too."

In the silence of the room, I watch as Theo closes his eyes, eyes that are currently flashing wolf, and taking a deep breath he pushes the wolf down. It's a full sixty seconds before he opens his eyes and turns them on us. Human eyes.

I let out a breath I wasn't even aware I'd been holding, until just now.

Obviously satisfied with his change in temperament, Bel moves to the side allowing him to step closer to us all.

"Thanks for coming guys..." Theo pauses and shakes his head as though he can't find the words to say. "There is no easy way to say this. So I'm just going spit it out, it'll be like ripping a Band-Aid off, painful but fast. The rogue vampire...he got Ruby. He killed my sister," his voice breaks with his last sentence and my heart shatters. Surely I didn't hear that right. I glance around at the others hoping I heard him wrong.

"Killed? Ruby? Are you saying Ruby is dead?" Paddy asks sounding almost mechanical, yet confirming that my ears aren't playing tricks on me.

"Yes." That one word hangs in the air. My wolf charges at me trying to get out. He wants to kill. He wants to tear everyone apart. He wants to tear me apart.

She was ours. We should have protected her.

He's right, but I push him back. I can't let him out now, I'll never regain control if I hand over the reins to him.

The room comes back into focus and I hear everyone talking at once. I can't even pick up on the individual words.

"Enough!" The order leaves my mouth before I can hold it back and the room falls silent. Theo takes a challenging step in my direction and I bow my head submissively. I should have never given an order like that. That's something the alpha should be doing. If she were my mate, it would be understandable, but I hadn't claimed her. Hell, no one even knows how I feel about her.

She died without knowing I love her.

I slump back against the wall before the weight of that thought can knock me off my feet.

"You love her," Bel whispers. "Loved her." Her correction tears at my heart even more.

I meet her eyes but don't need to say anything, I'm stripped bare. They'll all see it. On my face, in my eyes, in the way I'm being held up by the wall behind me. I can't hide it even if I try.

Both Theo and I choose that moment to ask each other completely different questions with the exact same word. "When?"

"Since...always," I reply honestly.

His eyes shift from me to Paddy and with a nod, I know he understands. He knows why Paddy ended things, he knows why two people who were once as close as brothers can no longer bear to be in the same room as each other. In fact, this is the longest we've been in the same room as each other without someone having to pull us off each other.

Theo addresses us all. "I received a call from Dominick, about thirty minutes ago."

"Domi—" Theo's raised hand causes the cursed name leaving Wes' mouth to stop.

"Dominick, found her body outside his compound. She was left as a gift." He visibly swallows the lump in his throat and carries on, before any of us can argue. "The reason I called you all here tonight is because I need to know who was with her last? Who was meant to be guarding her?"

Bel waivers on her feet, her knees almost giving way beneath her. "Oh God." She slaps a hand to her throat.

Theo reaches out to steady her before her legs fall from under her. "Sweetheart? What is it?" he asks gently as he wraps her in his arms.

"No, don't." She pulls away from his reach. "I don't deserve it. It was me. I...I was the last one with her. We went to the movies and I left her to walk to her car alone. I was too wrapped up in myself, and grabbing my last things from Misty's. I just teleported without thinking." In a hasty move, she turns and leaves the room. "I need to go."

"*No!*" Theo shouts as he dives for Bel before she can teleport anywhere. We've seen them do it a number of times before. Bel is a werewolf with druid blood, one of her abilities is to teleport at any time. Unfortunately, that means when she feels the need to escape she just dematerialises before your eyes and no one can stop her. "You will not disappear on me again. Dammit! We've had this talk before, don't run. It was my fault, not your's. I should've had you both protected. You're my mate, and Ruby...my sister."

Bel stands stock still in Theo's arms as she takes in his words and no doubt feels his emotions through her empathy, another druid ability. Their mating bond will be telling her a number of things about his words and feelings too.

"The rogue will be hidden from the sun for the day, so we'll meet at sunset to hunt him down when he resurfaces," he says as he comforts Bel in his arms.

Unsure what else to do I mumble a reply, "Okay, boss." As much as I want to find the fucker and tear him apart right now, I know Theo's right. He'll be impossible to find before dark, so going to hunt him down now would be a waste of time and energy.

"Guys, you know the way out," Theo throws over his shoulder, apparently dismissing us.

I leave the house feeling disconnected from reality, surely this is some nightmare? Ruby can't just no longer exist. She was meant to be my mate. My back connects with the brick wall of the house painfully. I'd been so distracted I didn't even see Paddy set his sights on me.

"She'd be alive if you'd manned up and claimed her!" he yells in my face as he pins me to the wall with his body. His anger travelling over me feeds my own.

I shove him in the chest. "If you hadn't broken her heart, she'd have been with you," I spit back the lie, knowing he's right but not wanting to admit it.

"You're a coward. You won't even admit your guilt. You're going to leave your alpha pair in there," he points an angry finger to the house, "blaming themselves when it was you. I broke up with her because she was yours. You should have claimed her."

The truth of his words and the anger I have for myself force me into action. My arm comes back and my fist flies forward connecting with his nose before he can block it.

Blood spurts everywhere. The sight of it doesn't make me feel any better, it makes me think of the blood Ruby would have lost in the moments before her death. Paddy's fist hits my cheekbone before I can dwell on that thought. The pain takes my mind away from everything else. The ache in my chest eases and I stand there, ready to take anything he will throw at me just for a little peace from that ache. The punches come thick and fast and I soak up the pain, I deserve worse.

"For fuck's sake," I hear Billy shout, as Paddy's punches suddenly stop. "Can you not see he wants it? He's not even fighting back, Paddy."

Arms suddenly turn my body and through my swollen eyes I can just make out Wes' face peering at me, he prods at my face and I welcome the pain it causes. There's a click in my cheek as he manipulates the bones back in place before they heal. "You're lucky it wasn't shattered to pieces, it wouldn't do your lovely face any favours."

"I don't care," I mutter. "Ruby's dead and Paddy's right, it *was* my fault."

"Give yourself a break. If what Paddy is saying is the truth, I can see why you didn't claim her. She was still cut up over him. They broke up what, two days ago? She needed a friend, not someone dominating her by claiming her. You and your wolf did the right thing, you gave her what she needed."

I shake my head denying his words, even as the anger I had at myself dissipates. Without the anger, the ache in my heart intensifies and I raise my hand to clutch at my chest.

"Come on, come back to mine for a bit, you can get your head straight so we can get the bastard tonight," he offers.

I glance at the woods and know instantly what I need to do. "No, I need to run," I've denied my wolf to come forward even a little, he's calm enough to be allowed out now. He believes the only person to blame is the rogue vampire, even if I don't agree with him.

"Okay, you know where I am if you need me? Don't be alone too long." Accepting my nod as agreement, he turns his attention to Paddy and Billy. "Did you manage to straighten his nose before it set?"

Ignoring the rest of their conversation, I head into the woods. Once I'm out of sight, I strip off my clothes and place them safely over a tree branch, to keep them as clean as possible.

Crouching down, I release the wolf and welcome the freedom that comes with it.

23. REBORN
Ruby

The noise wakes me. It's like someone's decided to take up the drums. But they have no rhythm. No, it's worse, it's like multiple people are having a drum off, and no one has any rhythm. It almost sounds like heartbeats, all beating at different times and paces.

It is heartbeats.

Concentrating on each individual one, tells me there are five of them. One of them is erratic. My breath comes in short, sharp gasps and I realise too late, that heartbeat belongs to me.

"She's waking up," a male voice shouts.

"Whisper, remember how deafening every little noise seems when you first come around," another male says much quieter, not quite a whisper to my ears.

I open my eyes to a dark room, it scares me for a moment and I bolt upright. A hand rests on my shoulder holding me in place.

"Take it easy, Ruby. You're safe now," the second male says. I relax and he removes his hand. "What do you remember?"

My eyes are adjusting to the light and I can now see the silhouettes of four people, two are close to me and the other two are hovering by the door. He said I'm safe, but how do I know these people didn't cause whatever happened to me? I guess if they had meant me harm they wouldn't be hanging back from me. Wouldn't they have killed me instead of letting me come around? I try to think about the question I'd just been asked. I remember darkness and tell them as much. "Darkness," my voice sounds croaky as if I haven't used it for some time. I cough trying to clear my throat.

"Can you remember what you had planned last night?" he asks.

I wrack my brain, trying to pin down anything. I have so many thoughts and worries going through it, I can't concentrate on just one. *My brother, where the fuck is he?* I'd somehow been knocked unconscious, why isn't one of his wolves here? There is always one following me. Why am I in a room full of strangers? I was with Rosabel, she should be here. The thought pops into my head and I remember.

"I was at the movies with Bel," I say excitedly. "We left. She needed to pack some more things so she did her little trick of disappearing." I can't think of the word she calls it, hoping they know what I was meaning, I carry on with the memory. "I needed to get to my car down the road. I was jumpy, but I thought it was lingering from the movie we'd just seen. Until I heard the footsteps behind me. I told them...told them Theo would be pissed because they weren't being covert enough."

The second male who seems to be in charge interrupts me, as I pause for a breath. "You told who?"

I think for a second trying to remember more. "Whoever was following me, Theo always has someone following me," I say slightly confused at the question, who else would I be talking about? I shake my head and allow the memory to flow. Not speaking, just reliving it.

The dark street.

The click, clack.

The vampire at my neck.

The terror.

My last wish of being a werewolf before nothing but blackness.

"It was a vampire. He was draining me. Killing me." Panic sets in and my stomach churns. What happened to me? Am I dead?

"Is this...is this heaven?" I ask in a whisper.

"Ha! Far from it sweetheart." A woman by the door laughs obnoxiously. The noise startles me and I jump back on the bed I'm lying on, pressing my back firmly against the headboard.

"Sam!" the leader admonishes.

"I'm sorry, Dominick, but you are babying her. I know you're trying to be gentle, but you're going to make it worse for her in the long run."

"Leave, before I say something I regret!" the male, *Dominick*, orders.

Dominick. I've heard my brother talk about him, he's a vampire. The female leaves the room leaving the door slightly ajar, allowing a little light into the room.

"I know who you are. Did you kidnap me to piss my brother off?" I ask stunned at the revelation. I carry on before he can get a word in, "Was draining me part of the order or did someone disobey the good king?"

The room becomes eerily quiet. I can feel a crackle in the air against my skin. I also hear Dominick take a deep breath in before I sense the power in the room dissipate.

I take a breath to question what that was, and the most delicious smell arouses my senses, making my taste buds salivate. My teeth start to ache and my stomach feels like it's on fire. I rub my tongue over the painful teeth and feel the points of fangs and I know in this instant that I'm a vampire.

A bloodsucking vampire.

"That smell?" I question, it's the only thing I care about at this moment, not what's happening to my body or why, but where that delicious smell is coming from?

"That would be me," the person near the door finally speaks. I watch as he steps closer.

"Wait!" Dominick stops him, stepping into his path. "We haven't explained things yet. She doesn't know when to stop."

"She knows what she is already, the look on her face says as much. None of the newbies know when to stop, but I trust that you *will* stop her before she comes close to killing me."

Dominick slowly moves out of the way, allowing the human to come closer to me.

I sit perfectly still, not wanting to scare my prey away. I don't want him to have doubts about what he's doing. I need his blood. I'm yearning for his blood.

"I guess I should introduce myself to you since you'll be feeding on me in a minute. I'm Jack, I volunteer for these first feeds because I'm good with pain, so don't worry about hurting me." He sits next me on the bed and I can't hold myself back, I pounce on his neck and take what I need. Taken by surprise he's knocked off balance, I curl myself over him as he lays on the bed.

The warm liquid running down my throat energises me, I've never felt anything like it. I need more. I pull more and more of the liquid. It's slowed its pace, but it's still coming.

"Ruby, stop!"

Someone pulls at me, effectively lifting me off my prey. I don't let go, but soon enough he's torn from my grasp.

"Take care of Jack. I'll deal with things here," Dominick informs someone.

I hiss at Dominick, I need the human back. I need the energy running through his veins.

"That's rather rude considering I'm the one that brought you the food in the first place. We wouldn't want to completely deplete our stock now would we?"

His logic calms me considerably. Feeling me soften, he slowly releases me and I sit back on the bed. He walks across the room and using a dimmer switch on the wall, he slowly brightens a light on the ceiling.

"Did you do this to me?" I ask the question I'd asked earlier once again.

"No, not in the sense you are thinking." He pulls out the chair, one of these office type chairs that swivel from behind a desk in the corner of the room and rolls it so it sits facing me. He takes a seat before talking again, "Do you know why Theo has upped his security when it comes to you?"

I frown and think back. "Yes, there is some rogue vampire, killing girls who look a lot like me."

"Yes, well, this rogue had been evading us for weeks. He's been leaving his kills for me, like a gift. Tonight I came home to find you on my doorstep. You were so close to death, the only choices I had were to turn you or let you die completely. I chose the former."

"Did you get him?" I ask, not knowing what else to say. *Does he expect me to thank him?* How can I thank him when I don't know if he made the right decision for me, or not?

"No, but this time he left me a message. So I know who he is and his motives."

"A message?" I question.

"He etched his initials into your face," he says matter-of-factly like it's a normal everyday occurrence.

I reach up to touch my face with a frown - feeling for these words.

"They're gone now, the transformation healed them, as it did any other wounds or scars you may have had."

I glance at the scar on the knuckles of my left hand, the one from a dog bite I had when I was ten, and see that he's right. It's gone.

"Who is he?" I ask, getting back to the monster who did this to me. *Monster*...I'm one of those now.

He stares at me in silence for a moment, presumably deciding what to tell me. "Since he took your life, I suppose you deserve to know, but to tell you his story, I need to tell you some of mine."

Hell yes, I deserve to know. I nod my agreement.

Having heard his name mentioned by Theo a few times, he looks nothing like I had imagined. His tight jet black curls were definitely not what I pictured. He's dressed immaculately in a slate grey suit with a waistcoat, but minus a jacket. It seems like he's been around for a long time, he comes across as old school in his voice, gestures and appearance.

He settles back in the chair as though he's getting comfortable. "I once had a lover, your brother would maybe call her my mate. We had a connection. I'd never believed in soul mates before but with Kathleen...I just knew it had to be. We were soul mates. I was already a vampire when we met, but that didn't matter she wasn't scared, she was more than happy to live in the compound and be my feeder. You have to understand this was a lifetime ago when I lived in Rome. I wasn't the king back then that came much later and is another story altogether.

"My beautiful Kathleen looked a lot like you, long blonde ringlets and green eyes. We were happy, but she started to notice her ageing, a wrinkle here, a grey hair there. None of it bothered me, she was as beautiful then as she was that first time I saw her. It bothered her though and she begged me to turn her. She wanted to be *Forever Young and Beautiful*. I put our request to the king, but he denied it. He said her spirit was weak and if she came through the transition she'd be lost to the bloodlust forever." His sadness seems to fill the room, I can feel it brushing my skin.

"I didn't heed his warning, I turned her anyway and ended up having to rip her heart out of her chest, which in turn was as good as ripping out my own heart. That night I vowed never to sire anyone again.

"I never fed from a woman again for a long time. I used men as my feeders and lovers. I didn't want to fall in love and if I stayed away from women, I naively thought I wouldn't. But what do you know, gender isn't really a selling point with me. It turns out that I'm bisexual." He laughs and gives his head a shake, as though it's an amusing thought.

"One night I fed off the most beautiful man on earth, to this day I still haven't seen anyone who could compete. Jay Dawes. My loving JD. Ten years passed in the blink of an eye and the dreaded day came when JD noticed he had crow's feet beside his eyes. He begged me, but with the memory of Kathleen and my vow, I denied him. I was king, I had no one's permission to seek, and yet I still denied him. Even when I could feel how strong his spirit was, I still denied him. When he knew I wasn't going to change my mind, he stopped asking, until one night we'd made love and curled up in bed for the day. When night came and I rose once again, he was gone. Never to be seen again." He shrugs his shoulders.

"Well, we both know that's not the case and with the message and gifts of bodies who look a lot like Kathleen, whom I had told him about, well, we can only assume we'll meet again and soon."

24. PEEPING TOM
Ruby

I find myself walking blindly through the hallways of Dominick's compound, thinking about his story hours after he told me. I have no idea where I am or where I'm going. I have a million thoughts running through my head. I try to focus on them all, hoping something will distract me from the burning in my stomach. I've been told it's the hunger and it will become more bearable as my body settles into this new form.

A vampire.

I've wished to be something more than human for most of my life, but to be a vampire. That was never a thought. Never an option. My family are werewolves, they hate the bloodsuckers.

I hate the bloodsuckers.

And now I am one.

My life has forever changed.

My brothers. The pack. My friends. They'll never look at me the same again. Dominick had told me of his phone call with Theo and his reaction to the news. I've lost them all.

I double over in pain as the burning intensifies. I could drain every human I come across and it wouldn't ease the intense pain. I'd just become a bloodthirsty monster that Dominick and his people would have to kill. I need to feed little and often as my body accepts the change. I need to learn how to control the hunger and only take what I need to survive.

I grit my teeth and straighten up, as I turn and start to head back to my room, a noise from further down the hall catches my attention. My stomach isn't the only thing that's changing, I can hear the slightest sound. I stand still and focus on that one sound that had distracted me, ignoring the footsteps and voices I can hear from various points throughout the compound, I hear it again - a woman's whispered moan. I find myself slowly making my way toward the noise.

As I reach the room the noise originates from, I come to a stop before the ajar door. As much as I know I shouldn't look, yet, I can't stop myself. My eyes fall up on a beautiful naked blonde woman, who is laying back on a bed, as an equally naked guy pleasures her with his face positioned at the apex of her thighs. I can't tear my eyes away from the erotic sight.

"Stop teasing me with your fangs…fucking use them," the blonde pants.

Obviously having done as he was told and used his fangs, the woman screams the name in ecstasy. "Niko!"

"I love it when you scream my name like that, Sam," Niko says in a gruff voice. "Are you ready to do it again?" he adds as he gently moves her up the bed and lays himself over her.

The thought of him feeding from her makes my fangs elongate and pierce my lower lip, but before I can mutter a curse a hand clamps over my mouth and the voice whispers in my ear. "Shh...They won't appreciate knowing that you were getting off by watching their private moment."

I turned my head to glare at the jerk behind me.

Cas, of course, it had to be Casanova, making a comment like that. Who else could it have been? His nickname says it all. He's one of Dominick's vampires, who I met just after Dominick told me JD's story. A good looking guy, the typical Mr Tall-Dark-and-Handsome, who looks to be in his late teens but could be any age. I wouldn't even want to hazard a guess.

He gives me a sexy smirk in return.

We silently make our way through the compound, and into one of the lounge areas. Once I close the door behind us, I turn on him. "I was not getting off. And if they didn't want anyone watching them they should have closed the door."

"The lady doth protest too much, methinks," the cocky bastard says with a knowing smile.

"Don't fucking quote Shakespeare at me. It isn't cute. I was intrigued, but I wasn't getting off. Okay?" I don't even know why I care what he thinks. I should just shut my mouth already.

His smirk turns up another notch. "I wasn't aiming for cute." He pauses long enough for me to open my mouth, but before I can let a word out he carries on with his argument.

"Your fangs were out, that's a sure sign you were turned on. Sex and feeding come hand in hand."

I can't let him win. "I'm newly turned, so I'm constantly hungry. My fangs are always popping out."

He looks at me closely, before speaking. "You do look peaky, when did you last feed?"

I glance down at the watch on my left arm. It must have been a good four hours ago, maybe even five.

"By the look on your face, I'd say you are well overdue a feed. Especially for a newbie. Let's get you fed," he says grabbing my arm and tugging me through the room and out into another corridor.

I try to pull my arm out of his grasp, but he's having none of it. So I let it be and allow myself to be led to God only knows where. If I get fed at the end, I'm not going to kick up a fuss. He knocks on a door and waits for an answer.

Within seconds the door opens and we are faced with a grandmotherly-looking woman, she reminds me of Gloria with her Greek looks. She's a human, I'm sure.

"Grandfather? I wasn't expecting you tonight."

I glance at Casanova, this woman must have him mixed up with someone else. How the hell can he be her grandfather? He releases me and pulls her into a hug. Catching the confusion that's clearly written on my face he reprimands her. "I've told you not to call me that, Elspeth, it only confuses people."

"I'm sorry, Cas, it's just habit." She glances at me and gives me a glorious smile. "Who is this gorgeous girl?"

Throwing his arm over my shoulder, he tugs me in close. "Newbie here is in need of a little top up."

"Well, you've come to the right place. Come on in and take a seat. I'll just go find someone for you," she says welcoming us into a lounge room. After closing the door behind us, she wanders off into what looks like another hallway.

"You heard the woman. Sit," Cas says as he takes a seat and pats the spot next to him.

I choose to sit on the sofa opposite him and ask him the one question that's been running through my mind since the woman, Elspeth, he called her, opened the door. "Are you really her grandfather?"

"Yes," is all he says.

"How?" I probe, hoping for more information.

Ignoring my question, I watch as he tilts his head as though he's listening to something elsewhere in the compound. "You're getting a treat tonight," he says with a smile.

Elspeth comes back into the room with a male following behind her, chatting between themselves. He looks to be in his mid-twenties, blond hair, blue eyes. He reminds me a little of Jared, only he has a more of an oval face with a longer nose.

"Tyler, I haven't seen you in a while. Where have you been hiding?" Cas asks sounding genuinely interested, as the others come to a stop before us.

"Dominick made me take a six-month break, you know how strict he is on overfeeding."

Cas nods. "Yeah, he doesn't want anymore Marys."

Elspeth tuts and shakes her head at the name. "Poor child."

Having no idea who or what they are talking about, I sit there in silence watching this vampire before me casually making conversation with two humans who smell ridiculously tasty. I never dreamt I would ever think anything along those lines. I'm looking at these people and practically salivating over how good they're going to taste. I always thought vampires were monsters who did nothing but drain people. Yet Cas isn't even hinting at wanting to eat them. There's no sign of his fangs. And Dominick sends them away for a six-month break from feeding?

My eyes fall on Tyler's pulse and I can't tear my eyes away. The sound of conversation drains away as I focus on the sound of his heartbeat, pumping his blood around his body. My fangs elongate and start to throb, giving the burning in my stomach some competition.

"Newbie!" Cas shouts, drawing my attention away.

Realising how awful I am for having my fangs out before we've even been introduced, I raise my hand to my mouth to hide them, while I try to concentrate on making them return to their hiding place. "I'm so sorry," I mumble around my fangs.

"Someone is hungry. Here." Tyler takes a seat next to me and offers me his wrist. "Let's get you fed before we worry about introductions." The look in his eyes, welcoming me. He's not emitting any fear, so he isn't afraid of me ripping his wrist to shreds, which is exactly why I'm not diving straight in. I quickly look to Cas for approval, he's not my sire so his orders won't affect me, but he's been a vampire a lot longer than I have so I feel that I need his agreement that I'm doing what I should. With his nod, I take Tyler's hand and raise his wrist to my lips. The sound of his pulse once again catches my attention and the impulse to feed takes over as I sink my fangs into his flesh and draw on his blood.

"Newbie, you aren't meant to be draining him." Cas' comment causes me to pause mid-draw. I look up at Tyler and take note of his pale complexion. I release his wrist immediately and jump back over the arm of the sofa and come to standing position about a metre away.

"I'm sorry. I..." I turn my eyes on Cas. "Why the fuck didn't you stop me sooner?" I snap, he should know better. *Why would he let me almost drain the poor guy?*

"Calm it, Kermit! You needed a good drink to tide you over through the day. I wasn't going to let you drain him, he hasn't fed anyone for six months, he'll be fine."

"I'm fine. A little...exhilarated," Tyler says as he puts a cushion over his crotch. The draw on a vein tends to leave the humans sexually excited, just as Cas said earlier, 'feeding and sex come hand in hand.'

"I'm usually more professional about feeding, the six-month break must've affected me more than I realised. You haven't harmed me, honest," he says with a shake of his head as if he could shake the evidence of his embarrassment from his rosy cheeks. I notice that somewhere along the line he's placed a cotton pad over the puncture marks on his wrist, as he's cradling it tight against his chest.

"He'll be back to normal once he gets some sugar and fluids into him," Elspeth says as she gets up and makes her way to a small fridge in the corner of the room. I watch as she removes a small bottle of orange juice and brings it back to Tyler.

"Cas said you're a newbie, but that can't be right? You seem to have a good handle on your bloodlust." I could hear the question in Tyler's statement.

"I was wondering the same thing, I've seen plenty of new vampires feed in my lifetime and not many of them are as neat at it as you were just then," Elspeth adds.

"She's sired by Dominick," Cas answers. As he pricks a fingertip on his fang, before leaning forward and pulling Tyler's wrist to him. "Here," he says as he rubs the droplet of blood over Tyler's still bleeding puncture marks.

I watch as the wounds close before our eyes.

Holy shit! How did I not know Vampire blood had healing properties for humans? Not wanting to look like an idiot I won't comment on it.

"Dominick doesn't sire people, the last time he did, it was centuries ago. You must be special to get him to break his own rules like that," Elspeth explains.

"My brother is the alpha of the Mount Roxby Pack, that probably has something to do with it," I admit.

"That explains it, he wouldn't have wanted a war between us and the pack, not now we've been working together. Theo and Dominick have been on the brink of war for years, it's only since the alpha female came to town that peace looked somewhat possible."

"For the time being!" Dominick interjects as he enters the room.

25. HOT TEMPERED PUP
Dominick

"Master Dominick?" I only rose a matter of minutes before Elspeth's words accompany a gentle knock on the door.

Elspeth would not disturb me at this time of the day unless it were important. I dart to open the door not caring that I'm only wearing my underwear. "What's wrong?" I ask the concern for my people bleeding out of me.

"I'm sorry to disturb you so early, but there's someone at the front door. He's furious. I'm not sure how much longer the door will hold against his strength." The door she's talking about is a reinforced door, it should hold up to almost anything.

I pat her arm to reassure her I'm not mad at her. "You did the right thing. I'll get dressed and go and see who it is. Go back to the human quarters, make sure you lock the doors and don't let anyone in or out until I come and tell you it's all clear."

"Okay, I'll round everyone up," she says before turning and leaving to fulfil her mission.

I throw some clothes on and make myself materialise behind the closed door. I would like to keep this outside, but it's still early and the sun won't allow me to keep my people safe that way.

Bang. Bang. Bang.

"You better open this fucking door right now, bloodsucker, or I'll knock the fucker down." The person on the other side threatens. If he's going to throw threats he better be willing to stand up to me when he's before me.

I open the door as requested and find myself pinned to the wall behind it. The door quickly slams shut, not giving the remnants of the sun a chance to touch me. At least he doesn't want me dead. Not yet at least. The hands pinning me to the wall don't ease up on their grip.

"What the fuck have you done to my little sister?" the werewolf demands.

Sister? Is it really Cain? He always did have a hot temper, he killed his father after all. "I do believe it's in your best interest to unhand me immediately, pup."

Cain growls at the nickname but doesn't loosen his hold. "One of your bloodsuckers killed my sister. They need to pay, Dominick."

I glare at him, in silence, giving him time to think about what he's doing. Coming to his senses Cain releases his hold. He's the polar opposite of his brother and sister with his jet black hair and deep cobalt eyes. He's the double of his father leaving me to the assumption that Theo and Ruby take after their mother.

"Thank you," I say straightening my shirt. "The vampire that attacked your sister was not one of my men. You should be grateful that I found her in time to turn her."

"You did what?" Cain growls, with a look of terror on his face.

"Cain?" Ruby's voice questions from down the corridor. We both turn to look in her direction as she races down the hall and into her brother's open arms. Her nostrils flare as she glances at her brother's pulse racing in his neck.

Seeing the look on her face, I rip her out of her brother's arms before she can sink her teeth in. *"No!"*

"What the fuck?" Cain questions, not having seen the look on his sister's face.

Tears roll down her cheeks. "You smell so good. I'm so sorry."

Cain looks at me, helpless, I can tell he wants to pull her into his arms and comfort her. Easing my hold on her, I allow him to pull her to his side, making sure to stay in reach in case she loses control again.

"It's okay, Ruby, he understands," I say, hoping my words comfort her, if only slightly.

"But he's my brother, and I can't even hug him without wanting to drain him," she says miserably pulling away from him.

"In time you'll have the control you need. Trust me."

Looking up at me, she stretches on her tiptoes and kisses me on the cheek before walking away, leaving me standing with her brother in the corridor.

Cain sighs and leans casually with his back against the wall. "Theo didn't tell me you'd turned her. Why?"

"When I spoke to him, we were still uncertain whether she would transition or get through the bloodlust. He was adamant that she wasn't going to make it. I don't know what was going through his head." I pace back and forth, unable to relax with the wolf so close to my people.

"They won't hurt her will they, to get to us?" he asks, as he looks in the direction she'd gone a few moments ago, obviously referring to the rest of my vampires.

"No, I sired her myself. No one will dare touch her. She's one of the safest vampires in the town. You may not believe it, but we are a family here. A lot like your packs. Ruby is a vampire, she's one of us. A rogue may try to harm her, but she's stronger now, she isn't the weak human you once knew," I say reminding him of her newly acquired vampire abilities.

He accepts my word with a nod and goes to open the door, pausing with his hand on the knob. "She may be a vampire, but she will *always* be my sister," he says before leaving.

I stand staring at the closed door for a moment. It looks like the Wilson pup that left town a lost little boy has come back a man.

26. CALMING THE STORM
Cain

While I was living the life of a lone wolf, I managed to find another wolf's missing mate. Frankie Rossi from the Rossi Pack in Western Australia. She'd been kidnapped and well hidden. My problem once finding Frankie, was convincing her to go back to her mate. We lived on the run for nine months, and then it was her mate's impatience that caused the reunion in the end.

As much as I had aimed to punish myself by living as a lone wolf for the rest of my life, after leaving Theo's life and marriage in a complete mess, I ended up finding myself a little pack of my own. I hadn't even realised it until I had to hand them over to their original pack. It hurt, so much more than it hurt to leave Theo and the Mount Roxby Pack over a year ago. Living together on the run gives you a connection like no other. When Theo called to tell me about Ruby, Frankie insisted on coming with me. Her mate and alpha somehow allowed her to leave his sight again, and I promised I would protect her as though she was mine.

When I went to see Dominick, my protective instincts kicked in, and I felt the need to keep Frankie well away from the vampire and his lair. Making my way back to where I'd left her at Misty's with Billy, one of Theo's wolves, I couldn't calm my temper down. Theo had made it sound like Ruby was dead, well and truly dead, when he gave me that nightmare of a phone call. To say I want to knock my brother's lights out is putting it lightly.

Storming into the bar, I let my eyes roam around the room looking for Frankie and Billy, ignoring the wolves that obviously recognise me with shock written all over their faces. Spotting Frankie's short spiky hair, I head over to the booth.

Sensing me she turns before I even get halfway there. "Everything okay?" she asks, the worried look on her face says she already knows the answer to that question.

"Theo made it out as though she was dead! I'm gonna kill him," I snap as I pace beside the table, the energy flowing through me is too wild for me to sit.

"She's not dead?" Billy asks, apparently confused.

"Dominick managed to save her by turning her. She's a vampire," I state. "Why the fuck wouldn't he tell us there was a chance? Dominick said Theo knew she'd been turned, making it through the transition wasn't guaranteed, but there was hope. Hell, the king himself turned her."

"I need to tell Jared, he's been trying to talk some sense into Ed and Paddy, they both blame themselves. Bel is just as bad, she was the one that left her to walk to the car alone. The tension throughout the pack has doubled since last night's hunt for *'The Rogue'* was a bust," Billy says as he stands, pulling his phone out of his pocket. He has the phone to his ear as he heads for the exit.

"You need to calm down before you see your brother," Frankie insists, tugging on my arm trying to force me to sit next to her.

With a shake of my head, I pull my hand out of hers. "If his mate is blaming herself, I need to go now."

After considering my words for a second Frankie stands and follows me out of the bar.

"It was nice to meet ya, Frankie. Maybe ya could bring ya mate with ya next time ya're in town," Misty yells from where she's serving behind the bar.

The short drive to Theo's is a silent one. I use the time to calm my wolf down, he's pissed at Theo for not telling us the full story, but he's willing to hold back and allow me to take control of the situation. As much as I'd love to give Theo a beating, he probably has a valid reason for his actions. *I fucking hope he has a valid reason.* I park next to a blue Ford XR6 ute and take the keys out of the ignition.

I don't make a move to exit the car.

Frankie reaches a hand out to stroke my forearm. Her wolf's omega energy does the trick at helping my wolf relax. Omega's are a special kind of wolf, there aren't many around and it can be dangerous for them to show what they are. "You shouldn't be doing that around a pack you don't know!" I remind her.

"He needed it," she observes matter-of-factly. She was right. My wolf had needed it.

I give her hand a little squeeze in thanks. "Thank you. Are you ready to meet my brother?"

She nods in response and we both exit the hire car. We reach the door and I stare at it not sure what to do, this was my home at one point. I've never knocked on this door, but with the way things were when I left I contemplate knocking for a second until I remember why I'm here. I turn the handle and walk straight in. I'm immediately flooded with an onslaught of memories, I push them back. I'm not here to deal with the past, I'm here for what's happening in the present. Hearing raised voices Frankie and I glance at each other, and with a shrug we follow the voices into the lounge.

"He's pissed and rightly so, now fucking stand down, Theo," a beautiful brunette says as she stands between Theo and Ed, a hand on each of their chests.

"That was a challenge, Bel! I can't just let it slide," Theo says glaring at Ed over the brunette's shoulder. *Bel.* So that is my brother's true mate. She has to be made for him if she can stand between him and another dominant wolf like she is.

"He isn't going to be the only one challenging you before the day's end," I state, catching their attention like I'd intended, all three heads turn our way. "What are you going to do, duel the whole pack. I know how much they love our sister, Ed here isn't alone in that."

"What the fuck are you doing here?" Theo asks as he moves out from under Bel's hand and strides my way, his intent apparent by his fists tight at his sides and the baring of his teeth.

"Do you really think you could drop a bombshell like that and I wouldn't turn up?" I growl as we stand toe to toe. "Do you really want to do this? Our sister is alive. Do you want to duel and make sure one of us won't get to see her again? You didn't duel me when I slept with your wife because you worried about whether you'd make it out alive. Well, I haven't gotten any weaker since I've been away," I threaten.

Frankie pulls on my arm trying to pull me back from Theo. The feel of her omega energy rolling over me, attempting to placate my wolf doesn't make me step back. No, it's the fact that my actions caused her to reveal what she is in front of a group of dominant wolves, that's what makes me back down.

I see the wonder on Theo's face for a second before it's replaced with recognition as his eyes fall on Frankie. "Oh fuck, Cain, what have you done? That's Frankie Rossi. I need to call O'Keefe." He pats his pockets no doubt looking for his phone.

"I assure you, my mate knows where I am and who I'm with," Frankie says, speaking for the first time.

"I sense the truth in your words. But..." I could tell he was torn, he wanted to call Jesse, but he didn't want to call Frankie a liar.

I pull out my phone and hit Jesse's number on my recent calls list making sure to hit speaker so he can hear me clearly. He answers almost immediately.

"Is Frankie okay?"

Frankie jumps at the worried tone of his voice. "I'm fine, Jesse. Theo just needed some confirmation that you know where I am."

"Good. Good. I'll be sure to send out a mass email, so it doesn't happen with anyone else," he says sounding much more at ease. "Take care of her Cain."

"Always!" I reply before ending the call and placing my phone back in my pocket.

"Something tells me you both have a long story to tell us. Who wants coffee?" Bel asks as she makes her way into the kitchen.

Theo follows her into the kitchen and he pulls out the mugs, as she fills the kettle. "Sweetheart, I know how much you believe coffee fixes everything, I just don't think it will even make a dent in this problem."

We all stand around the kitchen bench while Bel pours everyone a coffee.

"So, you're an Omega? I guess that explains the motive behind your kidnapping?" Theo says to Frankie, breaking the silence.

Frankie glances at me nervously and I stroke my hand down her back in a soothing gesture, before she has the courage to answer, "Yes."

"If I didn't know better, I'd say you two were mated," Theo says, with a sharp laugh. "Looks like you have a thing for taken women, I wonder if Jesse knows that?"

With his last sentence, I pounce over the bench top and knock Theo to the floor.

"For fuck's sake, when did this turn to the Theo and Cain show? Did you all forget about Ruby?" Ed yells, anger pouring off his body.

I feel Frankie's Omega energy fill the room and notice how it not only affects me as I release Theo and allow him to get up, but Ed calmly takes a cup off Bel and sits on the couch and relaxes into it, closing his eyes. "Darlin' I don't know what the hell you're doing to me, but please don't stop. It feels so fucking good."

He's right, when the Omega energy hits you hard like it obviously has Ed it gives you a high. Very close to what a human would feel after smoking some good weed.

"What is all this noise? You guys know I haven't been sleeping well and I need to nap when I can." I turn at the sound of Selena's voice and feel my heart almost leap out my chest as I find myself face to face with her and her obviously pregnant stomach. "C...cain? What...I..." Selena sounds just as tongue-tied as I feel. I left with the intention of never seeing her again. I'd heard she left not long after I did. I would never have come back if I knew she was here.

"Selena..." There's too much I want to say to her. I don't know where to start or even if I should. *What the hell am I thinking?* No, I shouldn't say any of it. I can't.

Frankie, obviously seeing something on my face saves me. "Selena, it's great to meet you at last, Cain has told me so much about you. Would you mind showing me where the bathroom is while Bel sorts these three out?"

Looking slightly stunned Selena allows Frankie to guide her through the house without argument.

I look to Theo, with no idea what to ask or even whether I want to know the answer to any of the questions running through my head right now.

He answers my unspoken questions regardless. "She arrived a few months ago. Her boyfriend had left her homeless and pregnant. Bel let her stay and as you can see, she's still freeloading."

Bel slaps his arm playfully. "Don't be mean, I don't personally like the woman but she's pregnant. She can't exactly get a job and earn the money to rent somewhere. Anyway, your mum has taken her under her wing, she'd kick up a fuss if you threw her out."

"Mum's here too?" I ask, last I heard Mum was a drug addict. I had planned to get Ruby away from her, but I stumbled upon Frankie and my plans had changed. Being reminded of Ruby, I get back to the real reason we're all here. I shake my head to dismiss my last question. "Forget about that, Ed is right. We need to get back to Ruby. Why didn't you tell anyone Dominick had turned her?"

Theo sighs and picks up his mug.

Bel picks up her own mug. "I'd like to hear the answer to that question too."

"I suggest we all take a seat," Theo says pointing to the couches where Ed is snoring quietly. The three of us join him and Theo explains, "You both know how much I detest those bloodsuckers."

"Our sister is one of them," I growl in her defence.

"Are you going to listen or not?" Theo snaps. I flick my hand in a gesture for him to carry on so he does. "When Dominick called me, his words made me believe she was dead at first. When I finally understood what had happened, all I could think was that if she survives the transition, she'll be a blood-thirsty monster, craving our blood the minute she scents us. She'll be lost to us. I'd be lying if I didn't say part of me hoped she wouldn't make it. And I hate myself for thinking that way." I could see the anguish in his face and hear it in his voice. Bel squeezes his thigh comfortingly with a hand.

"She's not lost to us, she fought the blood lust after scenting me, I saw it," I say hoping to comfort him in my own way.

"You saw her?" Ed asks from beside me, having come around sometime while we were talking.

"Yes, she looked well considering. We didn't talk long, she hugged me and once she caught my scent it was too much for her to stay and talk. Dominick believed she'll be able to handle it in time. She's only been dealing with the thirst for a day. We need to give her time."

"My baby's a Wilson, she's strong, she'll fight through it," Mum says, stepping off the bottom step. "Cain?"

"Hi, Mum," I say as I stand and quickly stride across the room. I pull the sobbing woman in my arms and stroke her blonde hair comfortingly. The woman I find myself holding together is far from the woman I'd once known as my mother.

27. BACK TO LIFE
Ruby

I've been a vampire for almost a fortnight now, I've managed to get a good handle on the thirst. I still have some little lapses in judgement, but I haven't killed anyone and that's always a plus. Most newbies kill at least half a dozen people in their first month. Dominick says I'm a natural - I was born to be a vampire. I was starting to go crazy being locked up in that compound. At least when I was under guard of the werewolves, I was allowed to leave the house. Cas came up with a way I can feel comfortably guarded and somewhat free at the same time, he organised me a barista job in the small café at the cinema Dominick owns. Dominick was grateful for the idea, he'd been trying to talk me into getting out for days. So here I am behind the counter wearing a little green apron over black trousers and a black T-shirt. I've been ignoring the scent of blood that's been tugging at me all shift without an issue. I suddenly catch the delicious scent that belongs to a werewolf alerting me that one is nearby. Glancing up from the coffee I'm preparing my eyes fall on Eddie. My stomach does a somersault that has nothing to do with the thirst and everything to do with the beat my heart just skipped.

"You're a sight for sore eyes, beautiful," he mutters as he stops on the other side of the counter.

"It's good to see you too, Eddie," I say. My taste buds may be watering at his scent, but the need to talk to someone I care about outweighs the need to feed on him.

"Hearing my name roll off your tongue..." With a shake of his head, he lets his sentence fall short. Another scent fills the room, it's enticing, but Cas catches my attention.

"Who's your delicious friend, newbie?" he asks as he sidles up to Eddie, making a show of breathing in his scent.

"Someone you don't want to get any closer to, bloodsucker," Eddie says menacingly before glancing up at me sharply, no doubt realising the elephant he just let in the room.

"Now that's not a very nice," Cas complains.

"Cas, leave him alone. You can take over the counter, I'm taking my break." Ignoring the insult, I lift the counter and walk through, grabbing Eddie's arm as I pass before dragging him to one of the tables at the back of the café. Cas would still be able to hear our conversation, but I've learnt over the years that there isn't much privacy when it comes to supernatural hearing.

"How are you?" Eddie quizzes me before our butts even touch the seats.

"I'm doing good," I answer honestly. "How's Theo?" Cain's been to visit me a couple of times, but I haven't seen or heard from Theo. Cain says he's okay, but it's hard to believe unless I want to accept having not seen him if he was okay wouldn't he want to visit me? If I accept that he's okay, I would have to accept that he hates what I've become.

"Theo is fine, Bel's keeping him busy with the wedding planning."

Now that, I believe.

"Are they looking after you in that compound? You can come and stay with me and Paddy if they aren't?" he offers, sounding hopeful.

Panic runs through me, I wouldn't trust myself to live with two werewolves. Some nights when I don't feed just before I'm out for the day, I'll wake up ravenous, I'd want to drain them. I couldn't let that happen. Anyway, Paddy is my ex, I may have accepted that now, but I don't think I'd ever be able to live with him, no matter how much my life has changed. "I like it there, they have live-in feeders that are willing to feed you anytime you need it. That comes in handy when you're a newbie like I am." I shrug shyly. It's strange talking about my feeding habits with him.

"Okay, but if anything changes, remember I'm always here waiting for you to need me," Eddies says before smiling at someone over my shoulder. "Looks like I'm not the only one that's missed you."

I turn looking for a familiar face in the crowded café, it takes me a second, but I finally spot Bel worming her way around the tables. As she reaches the table, Eddie stands to offer her his seat.

"I'll leave you girls to gossip," he says with a wink.

Realising he's leaving I quickly stand and give him no option but to catch me in a hug. I breath in his unique scent; a mix of pine and engine oil.

"Hey, what's this for?" he breathes against my ear.

"To remind *you* that I always need you," I whisper back as I loosen my hold on him. Something inside me shifts, almost like it's falling into place. Proving to me that just because I've become something entirely different, it doesn't mean my whole life needs to change. This man is supposed to be in my life. I have a life I need to get back to, and seeing the smile on Bel's face as she sits at the table watching our exchange, I can see she agrees with the conclusion I've just come to. She isn't a mind reader, but her empathic abilities ensure she'll be able to feel my contentment and happiness as I reach the conclusion that I still have people who care for me.

"I'll see you again soon," Eddie says before he gives me a kiss on the temple. "Make sure that dickhead looks out for you in that compound."

I hear Cas chuckle at the comment, so I look up to see Eddie glaring in his direction on the other side of the room. "She can take care of herself pretty well these days, don't worry yourself fur-ball." He doesn't bother to raise his voice knowing our ears will pick it up.

Eddie growls menacingly, catching the attention of some of the surrounding customers. "Casanova is a wind-up merchant, ignore him. It'll piss him off," I say hoping to calm him with that knowledge. With a nod, Eddie heads straight for the exit, without another glance in Cas' direction.

"Now I'm wondering, were you worried for my well-being or his?" Cas asks in my head. All of the vampires tied to Dominick, be it because he sired them or because they have pledged their loyalty to him and in turn each other, can communicate telepathically. It was kind of strange at first, but it can come in handy when you don't want anyone overhearing your conversation.

"Fuck off, Cas. I'll tell Dominick you're causing tension with the wolves, he won't like that. He's the only one allowed to antagonise my brother and his pack," I threaten playfully, saying it out loud for Bel's sake, as I take my seat opposite her.

"Vampirism suits you," Bel says quietly, before pausing to laugh. "Well, that's something I never expected to say to anyone."

I laugh at her words. "It's funny you say that. Dominick keeps telling me I was born to be one," I say with a roll of my eyes.

The smile on her face suddenly turns solemn. "I'm so sorry Ruby if I hadn't been so wrapped up in myself this would never have happened. I should've walked you to the car. I—"

I cut her off as I reach for her hand. "Bel, it wasn't your fault. Please don't blame yourself, because I don't blame you." Her guilt is almost palpable in the air, swirling around her. "I was his MO, he'd spotted me and wouldn't have given up on getting me. He'd have done it some other time if you had walked me to the car that night," I add and receive a gentle smile and nod of acceptance in return.

"Have you got any special gifts?" she asks sounding genuinely interested. It's known by all supernatural beings that vampires can have gifts. All vampires have compulsion; they can make people forget things or even make them feel things differently. That's how a vampire bite can feel so good. Some vampires hand down gifts in their sire line, it's almost like how blue eyes or red hair gets passed down in a family. I take a quick glance around to ensure no one is watching, before holding my hand out, palm up, between us and concentrate on the trick I've been trying to master. A tiny flame forms in my palm before flickering out.

"I'm still working on it," I say embarrassed at such a weak performance. "Dominick assures me, I'll be able to form and throw fireballs eventually."

She frowns. "I thought fire was dangerous to vampires, I thought it turned them to ash if it touched them."

"It does, well, all except the rare ones that have the fire gift. We seem to be immune to fire. I'm the only one Dominick has known to have this gift since his own sire," I explain.

"Well, Theo will be happy to hear his baby sister is safer than most," Bel smiles as she says his name. The love between them is fierce.

I pick at the grain on the table, absentmindedly. "Ted won't care, he hates me. He hates what I've become."

Bel places her hand on mine stopping me from digging a hole in the table with my nail. I forgot my strength for a moment. "He doesn't hate you, Ruby. He misses you. You're his little sister, he loves you." I can sense the truth in her words. But his actions since my turning has shown the opposite.

"He hasn't done anything to show that. Hell, he hasn't even visited me, not even once. Mum and Cain come every other day," I say, the anger evident in my raised voice.

"He hates *himself*, Ruby. When Dominick told him he'd turned you and there was a chance you'd make it, he couldn't see the hope in that, that everyone else did. He thought you'd be better off dead. And he feels so guilty for feeling like that. He can't believe he did, he hates himself for it." The pain of her words rip through me so quickly, I don't know whether it's because of how my brother must be feeling or the fact that he wished I was dead. Not knowing how to respond, I don't. "Please don't hate him for it, he hates himself enough for the both of you."

"He's my brother, I could never hate him. That doesn't mean I'm not disappointed, though. Not to mention hurt." Remembering back to the night I first rose, I didn't know if Dominick had done the right thing by turning me.

How can I expect Theo to think any differently?

"I can work with that." A satisfied smile graces her face. "Come back to the house with me. He needs to see you, he just doesn't think he deserves to."

Panic runs through me for the second time tonight. "I don't know if I can handle being in a house full of werewolves. Cas has been shadowing me, to ensure I don't lose control to bloodlust. Theo won't welcome him into the pack home," I explain.

Giving my hand a gentle squeeze, she reassures me. "We can handle one vampire, we won't let you hurt anyone. The wedding is next week, you need to be ready for that."

Cas appears beside us, no doubt having been listening to the whole conversation. "I think you can handle it. Rosabel here is the most tempting out of them all and you've been able to sit opposite her for the last twenty minutes without pouncing on her." It's his words that give me the confidence to agree to it.

"Okay. I'll meet you there. I can travel just like you now," I say shyly referring to her ability to teleport.

"See you in a minute then," Bel says as she walks out the exit, probably heading to look for a quiet place to teleport. It's not that you need quiet to do it, but can you imagine the chaos it would cause if you just up and disappear in front of a room full of unsuspecting humans.

"Are you going to be okay here on your own?" I ask Cas realising I'll be leaving him to deal with the shift I was meant to be working.

"I'll be fine. I'll call a couple of staff in and head home when you've left. I'm only here because you are." We both laugh at his honest admission.

"You're terrible," I announce as I give him a quick kiss on the cheek and dash out the exit, being careful to dash at human speed. Moving at vampire-speed can cause issues for humans watching too.

***

I materialise on the front steps, not knowing how welcome I will actually be. Bel made me believe I would be welcome, but I won't believe it until I can see it on Ted's face. I reach out and knock on the door, only my knuckles don't connect as the door bursts open. I'm pulled into a strong set of arms I'd recognise anywhere.

"What the hell are you knocking for, this is your home, it always will be," Theo says as he squeezes me harder than he's ever squeezed me before.

"I know I'm made of sturdier stuff now, but it still hurts when you squeeze that hard," I only half joke.

He releases me slightly before speaking, "I'm so sorry. Fuck, I'm such a dick. Everyone's told me as much." Letting me go, he puts his arm around my shoulder and leads me into the house. "Come on. Everyone's here. We're just waiting on Wes to finish work."

Stepping into the lounge, I was happy to see that he really did mean everyone. It was like they'd thrown a pack barbecue in my honour. Who knows maybe we'll pull out the cricket set and I'll be able to whoop their arses with my vampire-speed.

28. HENS, PENISES AND REVELATIONS
Ruby

It's the wedding tomorrow so the girls have taken over Theo's house, while the guys are running amok in town on Theo's stag night. I hadn't been back home since the impromptu barbecue a couple of nights ago, so I'm nervous as I materialise in the hallway by the front door. "Ahhhh," the scream behind me isn't a good sign.

I turn to see the one person that knows nothing about the supernatural beings of the world. Selena.

Great, just what I need.

"It's okay, it's just me. I didn't mean to creep in on you."

"You didn't creep in on me. You just appeared out of nowhere...like a magician, but without the smoke effects. How did you do that?" she asks as she looks at me in wonder.

How the fuck am I going to get out of this? At least she isn't terrified.

"I...I..." I have no idea what to say. I wrack my brain to think of something that she'll accept, only to come up blank.

You're a vampire, you idiot. Use your compulsion and make her forget.

The thought runs through my mind and I could slap myself for being so stupid, not thinking of it straight away. I move closer to her, making sure to lock eyes with her, like Cas has been teaching me, and I pour out my power as I speak, "You watched as I walked in the front door, gave me a welcoming hug and forget the rest of this conversation." I watch as her glazed over eyes focus and she comes back from my compulsion.

"Ruby, it's so good to see you," she says as she throws her arms around me and gives me as good a hug as she could with the massive baby bump she's carrying around. She's only at the seven-month mark, I don't think she has room for another two months if the baby keeps growing at this speed. "Everyone's in the lounge." She releases me and points me into the lounge as if I didn't know where it was.

The lounge is filled with half a dozen women. Misty and Lucy, who Bel works with, are both sitting on one of the red L-shaped sofas next to Alyssa. As I pause in the doorway allowing myself to get used to the scent of werewolves, Selena walks past me and sits alongside my mum and Chloe, on the sofa opposite the others. I need to push down the hunger that comes as soon as I scent a werewolf, being in a room full of them takes a gentle approach.

Pulling a bottle of champagne out of the fridge, Bel shouts across the room, "Delly, grab some glasses, I'm pulling out the good stuff."

"Sure thing, Bel." With a spring in her step, Delly bounces in from the yard and over to the kitchen away from the group of girls she was talking to by the patio door. I'm surprised not to find any more pack members here. Bel is fairly new to town, she hasn't really had the chance to make any friends other than pack, so I thought most of the pack would be here. Misty and Lucy are both witches, so Selena is the only one here who's totally unaware of supernatural beings, as far as she's concerned monsters only exist in children's fairytales.

Bel pours the champagne while Delly carries the glasses around the kitchen bench. Once she reaches the sofas, she places four on the coffee table between them. Misty, Lucy and Chloe all grab a glass. "I'll just go and get another couple," Delly says.

"There's no need, I don't drink," my mum announces, making me proud that she's still happily sober. "Being pregnant Alyssa and Selena both won't be drinking. So we have a spare as it is."

"I'll take the spare," I say picking the glass up and taking a sip to calm my nerves. I'm a lethal vampire, you would think nothing could make me nervous. But put me in a room full of people, the majority being werewolves, and I can't help but think of draining them dry.

"Ruby, are you okay? You look a little peaky," Mum asks, as she weighs me up with her eyes, concern plastered all over her face. Last time I was here for the barbecue things got the better of me after a while. I had to leave without a word after my fangs popped out and I needed to feed. When I say leave, I mean I dematerialised on the spot, heading straight for the feeders wing at the compound. Dominick found me a few minutes after I got my fill and threw his phone at me. Both he and Theo gave me a tongue lashing about just disappearing. Once I told them it was that or drain everyone, they agreed I'd done the right thing. So I can understand the concern on my mum's face now.

"I'm all good, Mum. Surely I can't look as peaky as Alyssa does," I reassure her, giving Alyssa a concerned look of my own. She's an unhealthy shade of green.

"Morning sickness," Alyssa gripes grimly, before thinking about that assessment a little more. "More like all day sickness."

"Ginger ale will help with that, and a couple of ginger nut biscuits," Selena announces as she makes a move to get up.

"Don't get up Selena, I know how hard that is for you. I'll get them," I offer putting my glass on the table, before heading into the kitchen.

Selena settles herself back into the cushions of the sofa. "Thanks Ruby."

I walk around the breakfast bar and into the kitchen. Seeing me, Bel pulls me into a hug still holding the half-empty champagne bottle in her hand. The cold bottle I feel through my tank top was a drastic difference in the heat coming off Bel. "I'm so glad you came. If you need to leave at any time I will completely understand," she says giving me an out if I need it, no doubt remembering my speedy exit the other night.

"Thanks, I had a little wobble as I just came in, but I managed to push it down. So I think I'll be okay," I say as I pull away. "Are you nervous about tomorrow?" I ask, leaning into the fridge and pull out a can of ginger ale.

Bel reaches a glass down out of the cupboard and slides it across the bench to me. "Not yet, I'm more worried about what the guys are doing to Theo right now. He better arrive in one piece," she confesses, taking some ginger nut biscuits out of the *'Cookie Monster'* cookie jar on the bench top. Its cry of *"cookies"* makes us both giggle. Theo is a big cookie eater, he loves chocolate chip cookies, so I bought him the jar a couple of Christmases ago when I saw it in the shop and instantly thought of him. Selena hated it, she used to hide it in the back of the pantry, so it's nice to see it on show and holding Selena's biscuits. She probably grumbles every time she takes one out.

"He'll be fine. Knowing Theo he'll have ordered them all to behave," I say with a laugh, pouring the ginger ale into the glass.

"You're right. He won't make it easy for them to have fun." She places the ginger nut biscuits on a side plate. "Come on, let's go have enough fun for everyone."

We both make our way to the sofa and give a green-looking Alyssa our ginger goodies, hoping that they do the trick as Selena promised. Alyssa takes a healthy sip of the ginger ale, as Bel and I both find a spot on the sofa to squeeze our butts in. I pick up my glass and take my own sip of champagne hoping to calm my nerves. These people are family, I don't want to be on edge for the rest of my life when I'm around them. I'm immortal, for crying out loud. After I had fled the last get together, Dominick assured me, that in time I'd be fine. I do believe him since a number of vampires drink at Misty's without draining the werewolves there. Although Misty probably has some form of ward or spell up to protect her customers. In saying that, if a vampire really needed to feed on a werewolf, they would do anything to get their fix. They'd probably attack before the unsuspecting werewolves even made it into the safety of Misty's. I know there are laws against feeding on a pack member, and serious consequences if we break those laws, but that doesn't seem to affect my fangs and my feeding urges just yet.

"Don't get comfy, I think it's time we start some games," Alyssa says around a mouthful of ginger nut biscuit, her voice pulling me out of my worries. "Okay girls, we need to go outside for the first game, *'Pass the penis,'* we'll need plenty of space. Let's make two teams of four. Selena, you might have to just be a referee for this one."

"That sounds like a good idea to me," Selena says as Chloe reaches down and tugs her out of the cushions of the sofa. "I'm not sure this beast I'm carrying around with me is very game friendly." She gives her ample stomach a loving stroke before waddling to the yard.

As everyone makes their way out to the yard, I take my empty glass into the kitchen and almost fall over Alyssa, who's on her hands and knees with the majority of her body in the fridge. "What the hell are you doing?"

She pulls out of the fridge just enough to look up at me. "I know they're in here somewhere," she says before ducking back in. "If Theo's eaten them, I'll kill him. Ah huh! Looks like Theo lives to see another day." She rises to her feet with a joyful smile on her face and a cucumber in each hand.

I laugh and point at the cucumbers. "The penis for the game?"

With a nod and a grin, she confirms my suspicion. "We can't play *'Pass the penis'* without a couple of penises."

We join the others in the backyard and can see they have assembled the two teams, Bel, Misty and Lucy are on one team; with Delly, Mum and Chloe on the other.

"Ruby, come and join us," Mum shouts. Having no issue with being on their team, I join them in their little huddle as Alyssa explains the rules.

"Okay ladies, this game is essentially a relay race with a cucumber as a baton. Only you can't touch it with your hands, it must be held between your legs and passed to your team members legs," she says, giving a cucumber to each team. "The first team to have all members complete their leg of the race wins."

Bel and Delly both get a cucumber in position.

"On your marks. Get set. Go!" Selena shouts from the lounger at the finish line. Bel and Delly both shoot off the line, they're holding back their were-speed to a degree. If clueless Selena weren't the only human here, I'd worry someone would notice. They reach the end of the yard and run back, Delly taking the lead by a stride. The cucumber Bel is holding is slowly working its way lower down her legs.

"I'm losing my penis," she shouts with a giggle.

"I'm sure Theo would be happy to offer you his," Alyssa shouts back as we all burst into laughter.

The handover between Mum and Delly goes off without a hitch and Mum is halfway down the yard, when Bel and Alyssa have managed to get over their laughter enough to pass on the *'penis'* between them. It doesn't take Alyssa long to make up ground. Mum makes her turn and drops her *'penis,'* the delay allows Alyssa to overtake her. The handover between Alyssa and Misty is quick and she makes it halfway back before Chloe manages to pass her. We fumble our pass and set off with the *'penis'* between my knees, which makes running harder, even with the grace being a vampire gives me. I cross the finish line with Lucy on my heels.

"Thank God, that's over. I need to pee," Selena says, getting up as quick as she can in her state and dashing off inside.

"We had a disadvantage with two human teammates. It would've been a whole different race if we had been able to use our speed," Bel complains, as my team jump up and down hooting about our win.

"The way I was running then, I could have done better than that back when I was human," I state with a laugh. I'm not even kidding, I was abysmal.

"Fair enough. The next game isn't as strenuous, so even Selena can play. Let's head back inside," Alyssa orders.

Lucy and I both carry our cucumbers to the kitchen dumping them on the counter and join the others who are huddling around something on the wall, just as Selena reappears from her pee break. Once I get close enough, I realise there's a theme going on with these games. There is a large poster of a naked, good looking guy pinned to the wall. He has a target where his penis should be. The words *'Pin the Junk on the Hunk'* are written across the top.

"Where the hell did you find these games? Did you do a Google search for penis-themed games or something?" I ask with a giggle as I turn my attention to Alyssa, who chooses that moment to hand me a penis shaped sticker.

"I've been to plenty of hen's parties, so I have a heap of penis games stored in this head of mine. No need for Google here." She winks.

As Alyssa passes Selena, she gives her huge baby bump a gentle rub. "I can't wait until I get to this size. To feel the baby moving must be such an amazing thing."

Selena holds Alyssa's hand firmly in place and smiles. "Feeling it like this is fantastic, but feeling it from the inside is indescribable. There are just no words good enough."

I stand and watch the moment passing between them as I suddenly come to the realisation that I'll never experience that. I'll never feel a baby move inside me. I'll never have a baby of my own.

A tear escapes down my cheek and I quickly reach up to wipe it away. Not quickly enough, though. Mum grabs my wrist and pulls me through the house and into what used to be my bedroom. It hasn't changed one bit. I begin to wonder if anyone has been in here since that night.

Mum's voice snaps me out of my thoughts. "I'm sorry, honey. I was hoping you'd have longer before you thought about the things that won't be part of your new future."

"I can't have kids, Mum. I won't be able to give you grandkids," I say as tears run freely down my face.

Mum pulls me into her arms and strokes my back soothingly. "You can't give me biological grandkids, but you can still give me grandkids. You can adopt or foster."

Her words run through my head on a loop.

Adopt or foster.

Adopt or foster.

I realise she's right, I can still be a parent one day. I just have to think and go about it a different way now. "You're right," I say with a smile as I pull back out of her arms and wipe my face free of tears.

"Good," she says as she takes one last look at me before turning for the door. "We best get back downstairs, they'll be wondering where we got to."

With a quick glance in the mirror to check I don't have panda eyes, I follow Mum downstairs, determined to forget my worries and make sure my future sister-in-law has the best last night of freedom she can have.

I briefly wonder if Alyssa has a stripper booked.

29. THE ROMANCE OF A WEDDING
Ruby

Looking at my brother standing in the fairy lit garden, watching proudly as his beautiful bride and mate, walks down the aisle is a sight for sore eyes. When things went wrong between him and Selena I never thought I'd see him happy again. I can see now that even in their happiest days he was never this happy. The love is pouring off him. Bel has been a gift to us all.

The wedding was meant to be during the day, but Theo wouldn't have it without his little sister attending, so the plans were changed and Alyssa went out and bought what looks like a million fairy lights. It's gorgeous. She's done such a good job if she ever gets sick of being an accountant she should go into wedding planning.

Jesse O'Keefe, alpha of the Rossi Pack, has flown over from Western Australia so he could officiate the ceremony, bringing his mate, Frankie, with him. He's a big warrior of a man, built like a gladiator. Even with his suit on you can see he's all muscle, his blond hair is trimmed short on his head. Frankie had arrived with Cain when news of my death had spread, but she flew back to Western Australia a few days later once Cain had decided to stick around, and Jesse had flown someone else out here to accompany Frankie on her journey back. Unfortunately, I hadn't been able to meet her before and even though everyone trusts me, I don't trust myself to speak to her now. I wouldn't want to have a mishap and anger one of the only alpha allies Theo has.

As Bel reaches us in her beautiful lace gown, with her brunette locks pinned up on her head in a fancy up-do, she hands Jared her bouquet before kissing him and her uncle on the cheek. Bel's Uncle Jack, Aunt Lilian and cousin Benji, arrived yesterday. The wolves are used to having Jared around, so they didn't seem to care about having an extra werelion on pack territory, which was good because Bel wouldn't have it any other way. It appears the lions come with Bel, like it or lump it. She turns her attention on Theo, the growl he releases in the back of his throat makes me think his wolf is pretty pleased with his mate's appearance too.

"Behave," Bel says with a giggle, as she taps him playfully on the chest.

"I'll take that as my cue to start, shall I?" Jesse jests, before clearing his throat and addressing the crowd.

"Friends, family and packmates of Rosabel and Theodore, welcome and thank you for being here on this significant day.

"We are gathered together to celebrate the mating of Rosabel McGuiness and Theodore Wilson, alpha pair of the Mount Roxby pack."

He focuses his attention back to Bel and Theo.

"Rosabel and Theodore, you've already claimed one another and started the mating process. Your mental bond has formed and with today's ceremony it will solidify."

Jesse reaches into his inside jacket pocket and pulls out a green cord and places it over Bel and Theo's joined hands.

"As this knot is tied, so are your wolves now bound."

So that is why Theo needed to trust the person who was officiating, he wouldn't allow just anyone to tie his and Bel's hands together.

"With the fashioning of this knot do I tie all the desires, dreams, love and happiness wished between you, to your lives for eternity.

"As your hands are bound by this cord, may your mating be held by a symbol of this knot.

"May it be granted that what is done before this pack be not undone by man nor wolf."

I jump where I stand, as the wolves all stand in unison and howl to the couple.

Jared and Jack both join in with a roar before Bel and Theo howl too. There aren't many humans here only Lucy, Misty and those that are mated with other were's, the way Lucy and Misty are flinching at the sound is proof that they don't frequent mating ceremonies.

Theo bought Selena a pregnancy spa weekend to ensure she wouldn't be around. She had complained about missing all the fun, but when Bel came up with some bullshit about how it would feel strange having Theo's ex-wife in attendance, Selena decided the spa weekend was a good idea after all.

Once the noise dies down, the happy couple makes their way hand in hand down the aisle. Being Bel's, Man of Honour, Jared follows behind them with Bel's bouquet of flowers still in hand. Wes, Theo's Best Man, and Misty, Bel's Head Bridesmaid follow behind them. Leaving Ed and me to walk arm in arm after them.

"You look absolutely beautiful," he says after a sharp intake of breath, before tucking my arm into his.

"Thanks," I mumble. I can feel the flush run over my face. "You look pretty dapper yourself." It isn't a lie, he looks amazing. But then again he always looks amazing.

I glance out into the crowd and see my brother Cain grinning back at me, dressed in a smart suit his tie matching the purple of our dresses. His dark hair gelled back smoothly as opposed to his usual just out of bed look. I hope he and Theo can sort things out between them. He was Theo's Best Man last time. It's going to be strange listening to Wes give the Best Man speech instead of Cain, but you can't sleep with your brother's wife and expect to be Best Man for him at his next wedding. I'm just glad Cain is here and they seem to be talking.

By the time we get to the end of the aisle, most of the guests are out of their seats and wandering around the yard. Bel and Theo are getting hugs and kisses from anyone that can get near them. Cain steps out in front of us and I release Eddie's arm.

"Thanks for being my date tonight. I'll see you on the dance floor." Eddie gives me a wink before making his way to a group of guys across the yard.

Cain throws his arm over my shoulder and pulls me into a side hug. "How are you doing little sis? Not wanting to sink your fangs into anyone yet, are you?"

"Now you mention it, there are plenty of wolves here. I think I could take a few drops from a couple without anyone noticing." I make a show of looking around the yard at the unsuspecting wolves.

His arm tightens over my shoulder. I can't help but laugh at him for taking me serious.

"I'm kidding," I say digging him in the ribs with my elbow. "I had a good feed before I left. I'm good, honest."

"You little shit, you had me worried." He laughs and pushes me away from him playfully.

"I've missed you. Please tell me you're back for good," I say as I hug into his side once again.

He gives a long sigh before speaking, "I don't know. I don't really belong here anymore. I ruined everything when I fell for Selena." Something in his voice makes me pull away and look at him. He fell for her? He doesn't give me time to dwell on that thought, before he carries on talking, "But I don't belong to the pack I made while I was away anymore either." I follow his eyes and see them trained on Frankie, she's looking at her mate, Jesse, sheepishly. It's almost like she doesn't know him like they were on a first date, but they've been mates for years. There's got to be an interesting story behind that look.

***

The chairs were moved to the tables and the reception went without a hitch. Jesse had brought Ben, one of his wolves with him, who happened to be a world-class chef. So needless to say the food was divine. Well, it smelled divine and everyone else said it was. As a vampire I don't eat food anymore. It's not that I can't eat it, it's just that I don't have bodily functions like I used to as a human. I can still chew and swallow, but after that it won't do anything, it'll just sit in my stomach like a lead weight until it decomposes and breaks down on its own. It wouldn't be a pleasant experience, no matter how good it may taste going down. Instead of looking odd watching everyone else eat, I'd offered to help Ben in the kitchen. I'm clearing the leftovers off plates as I feel a wolf's energy behind me, thinking I'm in Ben's way again, I start to apologise, "I'm sorry, I'm good at getting in the way," I say as I hastily scrape the last plate.

"You're not in the way," Paddy says causing me to drop the plate.

"Shit!" Even with my vampire reflexes, I don't manage to save it from connecting with the floor.

"I'm sorry, I didn't mean to startle you. I thought you knew I was here." He grabs the dustpan and brush from under the kitchen sink and crouches down to help me clear the mess I've made.

I pick out the big pieces as he sweeps up the smaller shards. "I haven't quite figured out how to recognise each of your individual wolf energies and scents, yet," I explain before taking a quick breath and carrying on, "I thought you were Ben. I came in here to help and I've done nothing but get in the way. I should've just left."

"It's your brother's wedding, you can't leave. They haven't even had the first dance yet," he argues.

I give him a grateful smile as I stand and lean back against the bench top. "Thanks. Anyway, what was it you're looking for? If it's more food, you'll have to speak to Ben about that."

He places the dustpan and brush back where it belongs with a shake of his head. "More food is always good, but no, I was looking for you," he says leaning on the bench opposite me. "We haven't really spoken since…" he breaks off not finishing.

"Since I became a vampire," I finish for him.

"No, I meant since…you know, me and you." He's referring to our night of lovemaking before dumping me the next day.

"Oh," I say sheepishly. "So much has happened since then, I didn't realise we haven't spoken in all that time…" I pause not sure what else to say. *What else is there to say?*

He steps forward and takes my hand in his. "I need to explain what happened. I—"

I cut him off. "You already explained Paddy, you're waiting for your true mate and I'm not her," I admit sadly. "I was devastated at first, but I understand now. I'd be a bitch to deny you what Bel and Theo have. We just weren't meant be." I give his hand a squeeze before leaving him there and heading back into the yard. It wouldn't do either of us any good to bring it all up again. What I said was the truth. I understand and I'm over it. We weren't meant to be and that's okay. He was my first love, but he's not my *for life* love - he's still out there somewhere and I have an eternity to find him.

30. FALLING INTO PLACE
Ruby

The first dance song, 'I'll Be' by Edwin McCain, plays over the speakers that have been set up around the yard. Theo stands and offers his hand out to Bel. "May I have this dance, Mrs. Wilson?"

Bel makes a show of considering it. "I suppose it won't hurt," she says with a playful grin, before taking his hand and allowing him to lead her to the space that had been left clear for the dance floor. He says something I can't hear over the music, as he pulls her into his arms causing her to swat at him with a laugh. He laughs back and elegantly sweeps her around the dance floor.

The song changes and out of the corner of my eye I see Wes offer Misty his hand, as Eddie offers me his. "Shall we?" Eddie asks.

I stand and take his hand, giving him permission to lead me to join the others, which I notice includes Jared, who's twirling Alyssa around the dance floor. "We shall."

Our eyes connect as he holds me against his body, swaying to Ed Sheeran's 'Thinking Out Loud.' I stumble, if not for his gentle grip, I'd be on the floor. I can't believe what I see in his eyes.

Love.

A look of love that strong can't be something new. *How have I not seen that before?*

Quickly sending me out in a twirl, we lose our eye contact. The connection between us doesn't fade, though if anything, it feels stronger. I can feel it through the way he's pulling me back against his chest. I can hear it in the beat of his heart and the sigh that escapes his lips as I place my hand over his heart.

Sliding my hand up to his neck, I pause to feel his pulse behind my hand. I think about how he might taste for a split second before quickly moving my hand around the back of his neck and gliding my fingers into his short hair at the base of his skull, as I pull his head down to me so I can taste his lips.

His hand holding my hip glides around my back, his fingers digging into my bare skin as he pulls me closer, it's almost as if he's trying to mold me into him. If I was still a human he'd be leaving bruises, but with my new vampire strength it does nothing but turn me on.

In our frenzied passion, the taste of blood breaks through my consciousness. It's the most delicious blood I've tasted, yet.

I freeze on the spot, but I can't make myself pull away from the magnificent taste.

Having no doubt he felt me stiffen, Ed pulls back breaking our kiss, taking the blood away from me.

"It was just a nick, it'll heal in a second," he says, probably in reaction to the horror that I feel, which is obviously written all over my face.

I make a move to leave his arms. "I'm sorry. I..." I can't believe I've ruined such a romantic moment.

His hold tightens, almost painfully. Not even giving me an inch to move away. "It was an accident, I got carried away and caught my tongue on one of your fangs."

I duck my head, so I don't have to face him. I don't want him to see the hunger in my eyes. With the taste of his blood fresh in my mouth, my struggle with not feeding on the werewolves has come back, double fold.

He kisses the top of my head. "Come on, beautiful. Let's get out of here. We need to find you something to tide you over."

I look up to see how serious he is. "We can't just leave. It's my brother's wedding reception," I argue.

"Sure we can. After that kiss people will just think we're going somewhere a little more private." He releases me and takes my hand in his tugging me in the direction of the exit. "If you're worried about what Theo will say, he won't care. He snuck Bel out of here the minute everyone's attention was on the groomsmen and bridesmaids."

On the way out I give the yard a quick sweep with my eyes, I can see he's right, Theo and Bel are nowhere to be seen. Alyssa throws me a wink and nods her head in the direction of the exit, giving me permission to leave, the look on her face tells me she thinks *'I'm getting lucky,'* exactly like Eddie had said they would.

Eddie quietly drives me into town and parks up outside of Misty's. "I don't know where you get your feeders from, is there somewhere you need to go? Or do you just grab people off the street?" There's no judgement in his voice, which surprises me. I know Theo hates the fact that Vampires feed off people, with him being Eddie's alpha, I assumed Eddie would feel the same.

I turn slightly in my seat so that I'm facing him. "I feed off the volunteer feeders at the compound. I've never fed from someone off the street."

Eddie starts the ute and pulls away from the curb. "The compound it is then."

It's only a minute later that he's parking in the alley behind the compound. I sit here in the car staring at the compound door, not sure what to do next. Do I invite him in? Is he even allowed in? Maybe I should call Dominick?

Eddie breaks the silence. "I can sit here while you go in."

I nervously bite my lip, thinking of the kiss we shared not long ago. I want more of that. I can't have more if I make him sit out in the car. What am I meant to do, go in for a feed and then come back out so we can make out in the car?

"No, I want you to come in. I want you to see where I live. How I live." I quickly shut my mouth, realising I sound pushy and expectant. He might have only been lost in the moment when he kissed me. He might not want more. I open the ute's door in a rush hoping to hide my embarrassment. By the time I'm out and closing the door, Eddie comes up behind me.

"I'd like to see it," he says as he turns and sandwiches me between him and the ute. Lifting his right hand off my arm, he runs it up my neck and into my hair, pulling it slightly to tilt my head enough to look at him. "That kiss back there, wasn't just some in the moment shit. I've wanted to do that for as long as I can remember. I want to do it every time I'm within arm's reach of you."

I don't need to hear anymore, I lean forward and take his mouth with mine, careful not to catch him with my fangs. I grab at his shirt pulling him closer to me, the sound of fabric tearing causes me to pull back. Shifting my eyes to the grip I have on his shirt, I see the fabric under my fingers is torn. I quickly release my grip. "I'm so sorry. I..."

He laughs a big belly laugh. "It's a shirt, Rubes, don't worry about it. Anyway, the fact that you want to rip my clothes off me is hot!" He throws me a wink before laughing again.

"Oh, shut up," I say playfully. "It wasn't intentional. I just forgot about my strength for a minute."

Putting his arm around my shoulder he tugs me toward the door. "I don't believe that for a second." He's such a big head, but he's right. I wouldn't mind ripping his clothes off. "Come on then, let's get you topped up."

"You make me sound like a phone that needs topping up with credit." I laugh, at how ridiculous it is that I need *'topping up.'* "I don't even know if they'll let you in," I say suddenly sobering.

"Only one way to find out," he says, stepping up to the door and giving it a knock.

Casanova opens the door. "You live here, newbie, there's no need to knock." He catches sight of Eddie and his whole happy demeanour changes. "You, on the other hand, can take a run and jump. What's happening Ruby?"

I sigh, disappointed that my plans of showing Eddie all of me will be ruined. "I need to feed and I wanted to show Eddie where I live."

No doubt hearing the disappointment in my voice, Eddie kisses me on the temple and pushes me through the open door, as he takes a step away from the entrance. "Go, I'll be right here when you're done."

Taking him at his word, I enter the compound and head straight for the feeders quarters, just the anticipation of where I was going made my fangs ache.

***

I find Eddie, exactly where he'd said he'd be, leaning against the wall next to the compound's entrance. "All satisfied now?" he asks.

"Not completely, I still have a certain itch to scratch," I say flirtatiously as I run my hand down his chest as I pass to approach his car. Feeding can make you horny and knowing that Eddie was waiting for me out here after things had got hot and heavy more than once tonight, has made me hornier than usual. I jump in the ute and buckle my belt as Eddie gets in his side. He starts the engine and drives out the alley, without a word. What I'd give to hear his thoughts right now.

He pulls to a stop on his drive but doesn't make a move to get out of the ute. "If I take you in there tonight, I won't be able to help but take you as my mate. I've wanted you for too long, there'll be no holding my wolf back," he says, his eyes flash to wolf showing me exactly how close his wolf is to the surface.

Mate!

I scramble to get out of the ute and take a few long strides up the drive. "You can't take me as a mate," I say as I pace back down the drive.

"You don't want me as a mate?" he asks over the top of the ute, from where he's now standing beside it. The hurt in his voice evident, it makes me stop my pacing and turn to face him.

"Of course I do. I love you." It's only as the words fall out of my mouth that everything falls into place.

I love him.

He's been there for me for as long as I can remember. He stood by and watched me date Paddy. He was a friend when that's what I needed after Paddy. He's given me space when I needed it as I got used to being a vampire. If what he's saying is true, none of that could have been easy. He must have fought his wolf for a long time. But that doesn't mean I could let him choose me as a mate. He'd be sacrificing too much.

"There is nothing I'd want more than to be your mate. It's just...you can't choose me. I can't have kids. You'll never have the chance to have pups of your own," I say, not able to mask the devastation in my voice.

Eddie is in front of me in a flash. "Plenty of people can't have kids, it doesn't mean they don't have kids," he say's logically. No doubt taking my silence as misunderstanding he clarifies. "There's surrogacy or adoption, or even fostering older kids that need a loving home for a while. There're plenty of options."

I fist my hands by my sides, angry at the world. "I'm as good as dead throughout the daylight hours. How can I ever be a mother, like that?"

He wipes a tear I didn't realise had fallen from under my eye and takes my hand before leading me into the house. "We'll figure it out. Together."

Closing the door on the world outside, he takes my lips with his in a gentle kiss. All the lust from earlier gone, only love and adoration in its place.

31. HEROES DON'T ALWAYS WIN
Ruby

My heart's first beat of the day startles me up and out of the bed. It does it every day, you'd think it would be something you'd get used to, but I've been a vampire for almost a month now and it gets me every damn day. Looking around the room I recognise it as Eddie's room, memories of last night flash through my mind.

My hands fumbling, pulling Eddie's shirt over his head. Our mouths breaking apart just long enough to strip each other naked.

After we'd spent the night thoroughly mapping each other's bodies, Eddie ran around looking for a way to block out the windows before the sun rose. I told him I'd just teleport back to the compound, but he wasn't having any of it. He didn't want us to be apart not since we'd mated. He was right about not being able to hold his wolf back. I didn't even think a wolf would be able to mate with a vampire, but it happened. I mentally reach inside myself and feel for the strand - the bond - tethering us together. I smile when I find it, but that smile soon drops off my face, I can feel Eddie, he's anxious about something. I quickly search for my phone, remembering too late that I didn't have it with me yesterday. I rummage through his chest of drawers and pull on a T-shirt and some shorts, rolling them up at the waist so they don't bury me.

Just as I'm about to teleport, I spot a note on his pillow.

> **Sleeping beauty,**
> **Theo rang while you slept. There's a lead on the rogue vamp. By the time you wake up, we'll have a plan. Come straight to Theo's.**
> **Tonight we hunt. X**

After a short detour to the compound to get changed, I materialise outside of Theo's house, not wanting to surprise Selena again. I don't know if compulsion would have any long-term effect on the baby. I open the door and follow the voices into the lounge.

"She's human, we can't use her as bait," Bel shouts.

"Bel, she's our only option. You want to catch him don't you?" Theo argues back.

Jared, Jack, Wes, Ed, Misty and Alyssa are all standing in the lounge looking at one another, probably hoping someone is brave enough to stop the alpha couple fighting.

"Looks like the honeymoon's over," I joke hoping to ease the tension. Everyone turns to look at me in surprise, evidently having not noticed me enter.

"The honeymoon hasn't even started yet," Bel grumbles.

Theo steps up to Bel and kisses her gently on the forehead. "The sooner we catch this bastard, the sooner we can go on our honeymoon."

Bel sighs. "She's my best friend. I don't want her to get hurt." She glances over his shoulder at Misty. "She isn't even blonde, how can she be bait when she doesn't fit his MO?"

"I can fix that," Misty says. She waves her hand over her head and mutters what must be an incantation, in seconds she's green eyed and blonde. She could almost pass as my twin. A collective "wow," goes around the room.

"I'm not completely helpless, I have a few tricks up my sleeve and I'll be surrounded by all of you guys. Please, let me do this, Bel. Let me help stop this guy," Misty pleads.

Bel turns her attention on Theo and he wraps his arms around her. "Promise me you'll do everything you can to keep her safe."

He looks her straight in the eyes, unblinking. "I'll do everything I can."

"Okay," Bel says as she steps out of Theo's arms and walks straight to Misty, stopping just in front of her. She tugs on a ringlet. "This is cute. If I'd known you could do that, I wouldn't have let Aunt Lil' torture me for hours yesterday," she says referring to the time she spent getting her hair done for the wedding.

"It's not something I've practiced, and it's easier to do it on myself," Misty says with a shrug.

"Just be careful tonight," Bel pleads. "It makes me nervous knowing we have to keep our numbers down, so as not to give him a heads up we're onto him. It means fewer people to protect you."

Misty gives Bel a friendly hug. "I will," she promises.

***

Following the lead that came from Dominick, we all gather in the alley he'd scented the rogue in last night. It was almost sunrise when Dominick caught the familiar scent, so we know he won't be far from here since the sun hasn't been down long. Misty walks down the alley purposefully, while we all sit back in the shadows hoping he takes the bait.

She passes a dark doorway and disappears with a blood-curdling scream. Forced into action, Dominick calls out to the vampire. "JD, you've been busy."

"I used to love hearing you call my name," JD says on a sigh from the darkness. He steps out of the darkness with Misty in front of his body like a shield. He ducks his head and makes a show of licking at the blood that's trailing down her neck from the fresh puncture marks.

A growl echoes through the alley. I can't pinpoint which wolf it belongs to.

"Awe, you're no fun," he says releasing Misty and shoving her at Dominick. No doubt having caught our scents and realising he's surrounded.

The second I step out of my hiding spot I see the recognition on JD's face. "If only I'd thought of changing you, I could have been fucking you every day. Is it just like fucking Kathleen?" he questions Dominick.

Ed, Wes and Theo all move to attack. "Fucker!"

I'm not certain, but I think the insult came from Ed. Wes reaches him first.

Seeing him coming, JD braces himself and punches his fist out, hitting Wes straight in the chest. Wes freezes on the spot and slowly drops his head to look down at his chest and the vampire's fist deep within it.

"Stop," he says with a whimper as he gives Theo a dire look.

Everyone freezes and the alley turns eerily silent, you can probably hear a pin drop. I don't even think anyone is breathing. Even those that actually need to.

"Anyone moves and I'll rip his heart right out of his chest," JD warns. By the look of Wes' wince, he must be squeezing his heart in his fist to make a point. "I know you mutts can heal quickly, but I'm pretty sure you can't grow a new heart."

Theo's growl breaks our silence. "What do you want?"

"To let me go, of course. I've had my fun in your town torturing my old friend, and I guess it's time to move on."

The energy in the alley steps up a notch. I can feel the wolves' anger running along my skin, but theirs isn't the only energy I can feel. Dominick's vampire energy has a different feel to it because I'm part of his clan, I can feel it inside me as well as outside brushing my skin. It makes my anger burn stronger. I feel my fangs elongate, making sure to part my lips, allowing room for them. I know from experience that it hurts like a bitch when you forget and they pierce your lips. Feeling heat in my hands I look down to see a ball of flame in each palm. It's the first time I've managed to control it like this. A fat lot of good it will do, I can't throw them without JD hurting Wes.

"You know we can't allow that to happen," Dominick proclaims.

"Dominick, think about it for a second. He has Wes, and he will kill him if we don't let him go. It doesn't look like we have much of a choice but to let him go," Bel counters, the panic clear in her voice.

"I can see that, but Wes is one life. If we agree to JD's terms how many innocent people will die?" Dominick asks, adamantly. I understand what Dominick is saying, but it's *Wes*. We can't just let him die.

"But—"

Wes cuts Bel off. "He's right. Look after Alyssa. Don't let her lose the baby as well," Wes' courageous words spur everyone into action.

The vampires arm pulls back.

Eddie and Jared both pounce for him.

"Go to Alyssa," Theo screams at Bel, before shifting in mid-jump for the vampire.

I drop the fireballs at my feet and dive forward catching Wes' body as he slumps to the floor. Patsy, one of the vampires, appears beside me as I bite at my wrist hoping my blood will be enough to heal him.

"Even our blood can't make his heart regrow," the sadness apparent in her voice.

"What about making him one of us?" I ask naively.

Dominick crouches beside me with a sobbing Misty tucked into his side. "He'd need to have a spark of life for that, sweetheart."

The alley fills with the howling of Theo and Eddie.

Dominick, Misty and Patsy stand slowly, stepping back away from the body.

"Ruby, step away. Slowly," the command loud and clear in Dominick's voice.

"They won't hurt me. I'm Theo's sister," I say with only half the confidence I would have had before I was a vampire.

"You are also a vampire. One of us just killed his beta. Theo isn't in charge. His wolf is. I wouldn't want to test his clarity right now," Dominick's warning tone tears my attention away from Wes' lifeless body.

I glance up to see Theo and Eddie stalking toward me, menacingly, their fur is covered with a mixture of blood and ash having played the vampire. Once a vampire has been ended their remains will turn to ash. There aren't many ways to end a vampire, fire or sunlight, decapitation and a stake to the heart are the few things that work, ripping the heart from the chest works just as well as a stake.

Realising Dominick may be right about Theo and Eddie, I gently move Wes' head out of my lap and place him on the floor. Not daring to reach up and wipe the tears from my eyes, any sudden movement could make them attack, I slowly back away from the body.

I watch as they start to lick at his wound. Understanding the dismissal, I gradually slip my phone out of my jeans pocket and call the only person I can think of that could help in this situation. He answers immediately.

"Where is he?" Cain asks, no doubt having felt the loss through the pack bonds, just as the rest of the pack will have.

"You need to bring a van, we're down Carver's Lane. Be quick, I'm not sure how safe the rest of us are." I glance at Jared, Dominick, Misty, Jack and Patsy, who are all standing quietly around the lane trying not to catch the wolves attention.

"Is Theo in control of his wolf?" Cain demands over the phone.

I consider his question as I watch the wolves with their pack mate. "I don't know," I answer honestly.

"He must be, you'd know if he wasn't." He hangs up after his words.

Looking away from the wolves at the others, I catch the moment Patsy teleports. "With more wolves coming we thought it would be safer if there were less of us," Dominick says.

I nod my agreement. "You should take Misty. Jared, Jack, maybe you should both go too. I'll be fine with the wolves."

Glancing between the silently sobbing Misty and myself, Dominick nods, before whispering something in her ear and disappearing in front of me.

"I don't feel right leaving you," Jared admits. Jack soundlessly backs his way out the alley obviously not having the same fight with his conscience.

Eddie's rusty coloured wolf lifts his muzzle up and growls in Jared's direction. I can feel his annoyance through our mating bond. Probably annoyed that Jared thinks I'm not safe around my mate.

Jared backs away holding his hand up in surrender. "Okay mate, I'm going."

I hear howling in the distance before the sound of a van's engine reaches my ears. I stand for another minute until the van pulls up at the opening of the alley. Cain reverses to get the doors as close as he can, it's a narrow alley and the van is too wide to fit completely down it.

Turning off the engine he jumps out. "What happened, Ruby?"

We both watch as Theo and Eddie howl to mourn the loss of their pack brother, once they stop, they gaze in our direction.

"I'll watch him while you change, clothes are in the back," Cain says pointing at the van over his shoulder.

They both pad over to the van and jump inside.

Knowing it will take a few minutes for the others to change and dress, I fill Cain in on what happened. By the time I finish and wipe at the fresh tears that are running down my cheeks, Theo and Eddie have both joined us.

"Come here, babe," Eddie pulls me into his warm embrace causing me to jump at the temperature change. Being a vampire I run cold, so it's a bit of a shock to be held by a wolf who runs hot.

Ignoring us, Theo walks over to Wes and gently picks him up off the floor, cradling him in his arms he places him in the van.

"Are you okay?" I ask Eddie as I lay my head against his chest.

"It's difficult to get a handle on my own pain when Alyssa's is being magnified through the pack bonds," he admits.

Taking in his sad expression, I start to feel guilty for having brought the pack into this whole mess. If the rogue hadn't attacked me in the first place, Theo wouldn't have felt the need to join in Dominick's fight with the rogue and Wes would still be alive.

"Hey. Ruby, it's not your fault." He ducks down and kisses me on the top of my head.

I try to take his words as truth, but it's hard to believe. "How did you know what I was thinking?" I query.

"I know you better than anyone. I know that would've been your first thought, but the guilt flowing through our mating bond is screaming it loud and clear too."

32. Broken Hearted
Ruby

Cain drives us to Theo's house. Theo choosing to spend the journey in the back of the van with Wes. The loss of such a good man is tearing everyone apart. I can't stop the steady stream of salty tears from escaping. I sit between Eddie and Cain and sniffle for the whole trip.

As soon as the door opens, I'm hit with a mass of emotions, fear, anger, sadness, terror, pain, so much pain, it causes me to cower away on instinct. I want to protect myself from that. Eddie gets out the van and holds his hand up to help me down. It dawns on me that it's all Alyssa's.

Is this what the guys have been feeling all along, through the bond?

I can't sit here ignoring it. I need to be there for her. Taking Eddie's hand, I jump out. We only manage a couple of steps across the gravel when the front door opens and Alyssa comes running down the steps with Jared and Bel on her heels.

"I need to see him," she screams hysterically, making it off the steps and onto the gravel before Jared catches her arm pulling her to a halt.

"Alyssa, please. You don't need to see," Jared pleads, wrapping her in his strong arms.

"He's right, Lis. At least let Theo clean him up," Bel begs, coming to a stop beside them.

Cain walks round the back of the van and lets Theo out.

"I need to, Bel. I can feel it, but I need to see it. Please don't stop me." She stops struggling, but there's no stopping the tears rolling down her cheeks. I quickly wipe at my own tears.

Jared loosens his hold, allowing her to go. "We're all here for you, okay? You aren't alone."

She gives him a small grateful smile. "Thank you." Steeling herself she takes a breath and slowly makes her way to the back of the van and to the body of her mate. Jared follows a few steps behind keeping the promise he just made. From the side of view of the van I have, I see the moment she sees him and drops to her knees on the gravel with a wail.

"Wes..." she sobs uncontrollably.

Theo crouches down and helps her to her feet. She climbs into the van and out of my sight.

Giving her some privacy I turn my attention to a weak looking Bel. "Are you okay?"

She grimaces. "Too many emotions," she says referring to her empathy. Seeing her knees give way, Eddie reaches out and catches her before she drops to the floor.

"Jesus, Bel. You need to get away from all this," he says.

"I can't, she needs us."

"You're no good to her like this," I say gently. "Let Eddie take you inside. I'll stay here with the others to make sure she's okay."

Bel gives a curt nod and Eddie guides her inside. I don't think she had much left in her to argue.

I turn back to see what the others are up to and find Cain taking sure strides in my direction. "I hear a congratulation is in order, Ed finally listened to his wolf."

My lips start to turn up into a smile for a second before I remember what happened tonight. "Thanks, but it's not really the right time to be celebrating."

Cain pulls me into a hug. "It's not every day you mate with a wolf. You're allowed to be happy." He gives me one last squeeze and heads into the house.

Alyssa emerges from the van and falls into Jared's open arms. "What am I going to do without him?"

"You're going to be strong for that little baby you're carrying. You're going to live a long life, so the part of Wes that is in you and in that baby can stay on this earth," Jared commands while rubbing her back soothingly.

"I don't want a baby without Wes. I can't do this alone," she cries into his chest.

"You won't be alone, sweetheart. You have the pack, and you have me too. I might not be a wolf but being taken by The Controller together a few months back, I look at you, Theo and Paddy like a part of my pride. That's why I haven't left to go home to the rest of my pride, despite the incessant phone calls from my father."

She lifts her head from his chest to look at him. "So you're staying for a while?"

He nods. "Sure, I'll stay for as long as you need." They both head toward me as Theo joins them.

I walk to the house ahead of them and hold the door open so they can follow me in. Alyssa pauses at the door and grips at her chest, before backing away from the door and almost stumbling down the steps, Theo's grip stops her from falling. "I can't go in there," she says, pain clear in her voice as she stares at the open door.

Theo turns Alyssa's body so she's no longer facing the house; I quickly step back outside and close the door. "Okay. You don't have to go in there." He sounds like he's trying to calm a wild animal. Just as the thought crosses my mind, I catch sight of her skin rippling along her arms. He *is* attempting to calm a wild animal. She's pregnant she can't change or she'll lose the baby. "Tell me why, and we'll sort something out?"

"I can't deal with the pain you're all feeling. He's my mate. I can't share the grief with you. He's *mine*. I...I just..." she suddenly stops making sense. Her skin rippling even more erratically.

"Alyssa, you can't shift. Do you hear me? You shift and you'll lose the one part of Wes you have left," Theo's commanding tone does nothing to stop her skin from moving. "Where do you want to go? I'll take you anywhere."

"It hurts so much, I don't want to live without him," she cries hysterically.

"Do you want me to take you somewhere?" I offer, thinking the fact that I'm not a wolf will mean she can't feel my pain.

She turns to face me with her wolf eyes, her face has even changed shape slightly along her nose and jaw. "You're pack. It's just the same," she mutters, with a shake of her head.

Jared steps up to her slowly. "I'm not pack or wolf. How about I take you somewhere?" He reaches his hand out and strokes the rippling skin on her forearm gently. I've seen the wolves try to comfort each other with touches like that over the years.

Her skin stops moving and she glances at him warily. "Your lion feels different to the wolves. It's comforting."

Glancing between the two of them, Theo nods his head as though he's come to a decision. "I'll be back in a minute." He moves past me and into the house, quickly opening and closing the door. It's only a second later when he returns with a set of keys and a piece of paper. "This is a pack house, it's only a small place but it's empty. You can stay there for as long as you need. Does that sound okay with you, Alyssa?"

She reaches out and takes the keys and piece of paper in her shaking hands. "Thank you," she says, her teary eyes trained on Theo.

"I wish I could do more for you." His sadness is evident in his voice.

She gives him a mournful smile before turning her attention on Jared. "Will you stay with me? Just for a little while?"

"I'll stay for as long as you need me to." He reaches out and squeezes her shoulder gently before handing her his car keys. "Go let yourself in the car, I'll be there in a second." She gives him a nod before slowly walking down the steps and to the car.

Waiting until she gets in the car and closes the door, he turns to Theo. "Are you okay with this? I don't want you to feel like I'm encroaching on your pack members."

"It's what she needs. Does it piss me off that I can't give her that? Hell yes! But I'm not going to let my ego get in the way of her healing. No matter how long it takes. Thank you, for offering to give her what I can't." Theo slaps Jared on the back, showing there are no hard feeling between them.

"There is one good thing that came out of The Controller taking us, and that's how close it made us. I don't think any alpha could invite another alpha into his territory, let alone his pack house for the length of time you've allowed me to stay. I have nothing but respect for you and I'll do anything I can to help Alyssa."

"You're right there! I don't think I can even handle Jesse staying in my territory for longer than forty-eight hours, and he's a werewolf alpha I actually trust," he says peering at the house where the Rossi Pack Alpha is currently staying, after officiating his mating ceremony yesterday. I can't believe it was only yesterday when we were all celebrating happily in the yard behind the house that's now full of sadness.

Theo suddenly turns his attention to me. "Rubes, if I give you the spare keys to Alyssa and Wes', would you mind grabbing some clothes and things for Alyssa? Even though she said you're pack, with your mating bond being so new and not quite solidified yet, I think you're the best person to go."

"No worries," I reply, before turning my attention to Jared. "Do you want me to grab some of your things too?"

"That would be great," he says, taking his eyes off a solemn Alyssa, who's staring blindly out the windscreen of the car for a second to give me a small smile. As his attention returns to Alyssa, he speaks again, "I best get her out of here."

Both Theo and I watch as the car starts and they drive down the long gravel driveway and out of sight. Ted places his arm around my shoulders and leads me to the front door. "Let's go and comfort those we can. Ed is lucky to have you as a mate, that's going to give him comfort at least."

I stop with my hand on the door handle and look up at him with surprise. "You're not mad?"

"No. Don't get me wrong, I never wanted you to get with the *player* of the pack, but when he told me this morning, it explained everything. He was playing the *player* because he didn't think he deserved you. He wanted what was best for you and he thought that was Paddy. He's a fucking dickhead for thinking like that, but I can't be upset with him for wanting you to have what he thought was the best. No matter how wrong he was."

I throw my arms around his shoulders and squeeze him in a hug.

He laughs. "You might not need to breathe, Rubes, but I do."

I quickly let him go. "Sorry," I apologise bashfully.

"Don't be, kiddo, I'm just glad you're still here." He opens the door and gestures for me to enter. The wall of sadness that hits me wipes the smile off my face, but it can't touch the small place in my heart filled with happiness from the fact that my brother loves me and is happy that I'm mated to a wolf in his pack.

My wolf.

My soul mate.

He was right there - under my nose, all along.

THE END

EXCERPT

Please turn the page for an excerpt of

Reclaiming the One, Book 3 of *The Mount Roxby Series*.

Coming late 2016

1. INVITATION HOME
Cain

Leaving Ruby with Theo, Alyssa and Jared, outside, I enter the house. It shocks me to feel such an intense wave of emotion coming from the pack members, hit me. I don't know why I'm surprised? Wes was Theo's beta, he was well loved. Of course, the pack are going to be cut up about his death and they are going to feel the loss for a long time.

Theo's been on edge ever since I turned up, he doesn't need to be stressing about the past when he's got this hole in his pack to worry about. I came here to see what happened to my little sister. She's safe, happy and mated to a wolf I have a hell of a lot of respect for. Nothing is keeping me here anymore. Selena's name runs through my mind, but I push it back into the crevice it had been hiding in before. I ruined her life a long time ago. When I saw her the day I arrived, she looked like she was in a good place, looking to the future with her baby. I'm not going to spoil that. The best thing for everyone is for me to pack my bag and leave.

I make my way upstairs and throw my stuff together. It doesn't take me long because I didn't bring much with me. I'm a metre away from the front door when it pops open, Theo waves Ruby in before him and closes the door. I can pinpoint the exact moment the wall of sadness hits them, Ruby loses her smile and Theo takes a deep breath and looks around. Probably looking for someone to comfort. That's when he spots me and my bag. Anger radiates from him.

"My office now!" he orders before marching off in the direction of his office.

I'm suddenly transported back in time to when Theo and I had been ordered into Dad's office as kids. We were always getting in trouble and we were as thick as thieves, though. So we'd both claim to be the one at fault and he'd punish us both saying, "You both deserve it. One of you is lying and one of you did it." Sometimes he'd punish us for nothing, he did it to *'make us stronger.'* He was a prick like that. It backfired on him in the end because it did make us stronger. Strong enough to kill him and take over the pack.

Theo is standing with his back to me as I walk in the door, he's looking out the window overlooking the backyard. I close the door and stand in silence watching him, wondering what he's thinking? What he's going to say?

"Were you going to say goodbye? Or were you going to leave another gaping hole? Do you not think the pack has lost enough tonight?" He sounds calm and collected, but I can tell by the fisted hands at his sides, that he's pissed.

I join him at the window and sigh as I take in the view of the forest, remembering what it was like to run in those trees. The freedom you could find in there. "I didn't think you needed to be reminded of the past, when you have enough of the present to worry about," I say honestly.

He turns his head sharp to look at me.

"I know you hate me for what I did, and to be honest, I don't blame you. I don't expect you to forgive me," I admit.

"What is it with my siblings thinking I hate them? I must be one nasty bastard. I don't hate you Cain, I never did." He rubs at his brows with his fingertips. "You hurt me, you slept with my wife and then you went AWOL. You pissed me off, but you're my brother. I'd never be able to hate you." He sighs. "I fucking love you, you moron," he admits. Catching me off guard he manages to pull me into a headlock and knuckle my hair.

"Jesus, Theo, what are you? Fucking ten?" We both laugh and for a second. I forget about the hand the pack was dealt tonight, forget the loss we all feel. We both suddenly fall silent, looking to the backyard once again remembering tonight's events.

"Please stay, Cain. I need a beta who isn't so emotionally affected by the loss of Wes. Someone who can help glue the pack together while they come to terms with it. I need you, Cain."

I glance across at him not believing those words came from his mouth. "What about Ed or Billy? They're both dominant enough to be your beta. Ed seems stronger now he's mated. I haven't been around the pack for over a year, they'll never accept me as their beta."

"I'm not the only one that missed you when you left. I think you'll be surprised how many of them will be happy to have you back," he says as he walks to his desk and pulls out a bottle of whisky and two short glasses. "I know things between the two of us are strained." He pours two glasses and hands me one. "But I trust you with the pack, it's your pack as much as it is mine."

I down the liquid fire before I speak, "After everything I've done, you still feel like that?" I'm shocked to say the least.

"I don't know why you did what you did, but I know it wasn't out of malice. That isn't you, never was." He grabs the bottle and tops up our glasses again.

"I need to tell you everything that lead to me sleeping with Selena, and if you still want me to be your beta after that I'll do it."

He takes a seat on the sofa at the side of the room, places the whisky bottle by his feet and gestures for me to join him. "Now's as good a time as any."

So I sit down and tell him everything, starting at the very beginning. The day *she* came into my life.

COMING SOON

Releasing the Wolf, book one of *The Rossi Pack Series*.

This is Jesse and Frankie's story and it will be released early 2016.

ACKNOWLEDGEMENTS

I want to thank *my family* for supporting my unconditionally, for sticking with me and understanding when my scatterbrained mind forgets everything. I can remember what happens to my characters but I can't remember when I'm meant to be taking someone to their swimming lesson. I love you all to pieces.

Sara Cartwright, thank you for the amazing cover. You seem to get exactly what I am aiming for. I'm sorry you had to resize it a few times. You're a trooper for doing it again and again.

Kaylene Osborn from Swish Design & Editing. You made the editing process so easy and fairly painless. Thank you for explaining why I shouldn't do something rather than just saying don't do that.

Now for one of the most supportive people on the planet. This woman has been amazing, she's always there cheering me on from across the world, always sending me just the right inspirational messages. *Kia B-Stone*, I love your guts big time. I'm so grateful for our friendship. To show you how thankful I am, I'm announcing right here that Jared is all yours. Thank you for everything.

Sam Destiny and *Yvi Meissner*, thank you for beta reading for me. You girls are amazing.

Finally I'd like to thank you guys, the readers. Your support and love for Pride to Pack has kept me writing when I hit rock bottom and thought I couldn't do it. Thank you for being patient with me, and waiting, I know it was a while. Your messages telling me how excited you are for this book, has made the hard work so worth while. I love my stories and characters but knowing that you guys love them too means the world to me. Thank YOU.

ABOUT THE AUTHOR

Aimie is a Yorkshire lass living in Western Australia. She is a mother to three boisterous boys, you could say four, if you add her husband.

Aimie loves to people watch, it's her favourite way to come up with new characters and stories. So next time a stranger is staring at you in the street don't panic, they could be an author basing a character on you.

Aimie has always loved to read and write. Her favourite place to listen to her characters is at the beach.

Aimie would love to hear from you. Comments and questions are always welcome. You can reach her at aimiejennison@gmail.com or through her website http://www.aimiejennison.com. Thanks in advance for your correspondence.

You can also connect with Aimie online via
Facebook * Twitter * Goodreads

OTHER BOOKS
By Aimie Jennison

Mount Roxby Series
Pride to Pack
Book 1 of the Mount Roxby Series

Rosabel McGuiness, orphaned Werewolf, has finally decided to leave the Werelion Pride she's been living with for the last eighteen years. She's been challenged to one duel too many. It's time to find a pack to call home.

Theodore Wilson, Alpha of the Mount Roxby Pack, has never cared about finding his Mate. He swore off women when his Wife, a human who knew nothing about what he was, cheated on him. But now a new wolf has walked into town, and stirred up feelings he never imagined he would feel.

Mount Roxby has a plethora of supernatural beings, unbeknownst to the humans that live there. After a series of mysterious disappearances, and fatal attacks on both Werewolves and Vampires alike, Rosabel decides something needs to be done. But can she persuade the Pack Alpha and Vampire King, to put old prejudices behind them long enough to work together, and solve these attacks? Or will one bite too many cause a war?

OTHER BOOKS
By Aimie Jennison

Stud Mafia Series
The Don: Sebastiano
Book 1 of the Stud Mafia Series

Warning: This book contains violence, excessive language, and strong sexual content. It's intended to be read by mature audiences

Sierra Winters never planned on falling for the most powerful man in Sydney.

One minute, she's an everyday twenty-eight-year-old, working class office girl. The next, she's being blackmailed by Sebastiano Morassi, Sydney's influential crime family boss, to settle her brother's debts.

Sierra knows she should never have gone to him to 'save' her brother but she is captivated by him. His monstrous size, his malicious evil glare and more frightening is the scar, which marks his left cheek. Never has she met or seen anyone like him. The more time she spends with this frightening yet captivating man, the harder it becomes to want to escape.

Sebastiano Morassi is pure danger. So why does she crave him? He can make her tremble with fear and make her hairs stand on end, but he also has a sweetness to him, which tugs at her heart. Sierra soon finds herself merged into his world full of murder, revenge, and deceit.

OTHER BOOKS
By Aimie Jennison

Stud Mafia Series
The Capo: Riccardo
Book 2 of the Stud Mafia Series

Warning: This book contains violence, excessive language, and strong sexual content. It's intended to be read by mature audiences

Temptation. Seduction. Forbidden pleasure.

As the right-hand man to The Don, Riccardo Rossi's role is all about duty, respect and honour. Being the crime boss's daughter, Lorena Morassi is forbidden. Although she is young and off limits, that doesn't stop Riccardo from wanting her. She is a pure temptation, and to have her would be a betrayal to his boss and his mafia family.

Lorena has wanted Riccardo for years and she knows he wants her, too. Being with him would only cause bad blood between her father and his right-hand man. She doesn't want their strong friendship to be ruined, but her feelings for him grow, and Lorena knows she can't stay away. But a night of seduction and forbidden pleasure changes everything.

Betrayal will not be tolerated and long-standing friendships will be broken.

Visit www.aimiejennison.com to learn more about Aimie Jennison

Printed in Australia
AUOC02n0650220915
270450AU00001B/3/P